To Mrs. York,
Enjoy the
now!
With love,
Tracy

Tiger Hunting

A novel

Tracy Million Simmons

Copyright © 2013 Tracy Million Simmons

Cover Art by Maddie Simmons, Evie Simmons and Mackenzie Meier

This is a work of fiction. While some locations are based on real places, all characters and events are the results of the author's imagination. Any resemblance to real persons, living or dead, is purely coincidental.

All rights reserved.

ISBN: 1482687011
ISBN-13: 978-1482687019

*For Melissa Morrow Goldsberry,
a forever friend
regardless of the time or distance that separates us.*

Acknowledgments

I owe so much to so many people; to properly put it all in printed word would take more pages than this, my first finished novel. At the top of the list, I must thank Cheryl Unruh for the writerly chats that have helped me stay centered and focused even through times when my pen has remained far from actual paper. I would also like to thank Kevin Rabas for his infectious enthusiasm and optimism that we can all be published writers, as well as Wendy Devilbiss, Mike Graves, Bob Grover, Leonard Biggs and Jerilynn Henrikson of the very informal (but effective for me, at least) Emporia Writers Group.

My sister, Diane Million, deserves a book all her own as she is often my first reader, as well as my biggest cheerleader.

To my mother, Evelyn Reaujean Skaggs Million, I owe thanks for instilling in me a deep love of books and storytelling at an early age. And to my dad, Duane Million, I thank you for continuing to ask over the years, "Is that novel done yet?"

I would not have gotten this far without my many friends, acquaintances (and acquaintances who are becoming friends) in the Kansas Authors Club. I collect your stories in bits and pieces, year-by-year, as conventions and KAC board meetings and district meetings allow, as avidly as I read the stories you write. You have become my touch points in this great state of Kansas.

Thinking about my life's path to writing, I must also take a moment to acknowledge Clyde Goff, Phyllis Wipf, Rose Klenke, Laura York Guy, Callie Lyons, Derek Simmons, Melissa McLoughlin, and Caryn Mirriam-Goldberg. And of course there's a shout out owed to Amanda Jane Robb Neece, because whatever I do in life, your presence is there.

A page of acknowledgment would never be complete, of course, without mention of my best friend in the whole world (aka the most supportive hubby on the planet). Rand Simmons has spent more of the past 22 years believing in me than I have spent believing in myself. Thanks for the encouragement, bubs. You are the best.

To my children – Evie, Maddie and Kaman – you have no idea how thankful I am to be the mother of the most awesome-sauce kids in town. Without you, I might still be out there hunting my own white tiger.

Chapter 1

I should have taken it as a sign when I saw the dolphin lying by the side of the highway. It was western Kansas, after all, where it would have been odd to see water in the river, never mind a marine animal stranded outside of one. I was admiring the sunset, the endless expanse of horizon covered in swooshes of reds, purples, and blues as I drove the final half hour home. I was exhausted, having left Houston fourteen hours earlier. I'd stopped only three times for bathroom breaks and to buy more junk food, plus a short stop in Norman, Oklahoma just to stretch my legs.

When I first saw the dolphin, I was certain my eyes were playing tricks on me. Surely it was a calf or a large coyote. Perhaps someone's horse had gotten hit on the road. I slowed, the swirl of emergency lights and confusion ahead a visual cacophony that overloaded my senses. There was a girl with long black hair and a colorful skirt that billowed in the breeze. She was running toward the dolphin. I was close enough to see that her feet were bare. Gold bangles on her ankles and wrists reflected the lights of the traffic and emergency vehicles. I wanted to stop, to inspect the dolphin with my full range of senses, but an officer was waving me forward with a glowing orange stick.

A very small man strolled the white line of the highway. He lifted his chin and looked me in the eye as my car rolled past. His sorrow seemed to leap the space between us. I felt my throat close and I blinked away tears. I watched him in my rearview mirror as he knelt beside the dolphin. He patted her. His head dipped down and I imagined him curling up beside her on the ground with his sorrow.

"Meenling Acrobats and Marvelous Menagerie," the gold letters on the trucks parked alongside the road spelled out. A giraffe poked her head out of a tall cage in the last vehicle in the line. I counted six big trucks total, the first with its nose deep in the ditch. Beyond that, in the field, I could see the wheels of one more truck lying on its side.

Men were running, appearing and disappearing where headlights began and ended. A large ape stood near the tipped vehicle. Policemen with glowing orange sticks continued to motion the passing cars forward. I was part of a dense line now. I heard the roar of a big cat. The hairs stood up on the backs of my arms.

Soon the road was clear again. The traffic began to pick up speed. I kept glancing in my rearview mirror, assuring myself that the circus trucks and lights really did exist and that it wasn't just a dream or a hallucination brought on by too many hours behind the wheel. Even as I turned onto Comanche Street, coasting back in time as the houses on the street of my childhood popped into view, I kept picturing that dolphin.

"Fish out of water; but dolphins aren't fish," I said as I pulled into my parents' driveway. The porch light was on. Mom expected I would drive all the way.

I turned off the motor and sat for a moment, still puzzling over what I had seen on the highway, just on the outskirts of Dodge City, my hometown.

"Welcome home, Jeni Renzelmen," I said as I stepped out of the car. I looked into the back seat which was piled high with all of my earthly belongings. The trunk was jammed to capacity, as well. I went around to the passenger's side and pulled my large backpack from its crevice. The backpack wouldn't prompt any questions. I had purposely packed it like an overnight bag before I left Houston this morning. I heaved it up over one shoulder and by-passed the front door, entering the house through the side door as I had all of my life, as if I still lived here rather than just visiting.

"Jeni?" Mom's voice called from the kitchen. "Is that you, Jeni? Are you home?"

"Mom, you won't believe what I saw on the way into town. Circus trucks. There's been a wreck. There was a dolphin lying by the side of the road."

Mom was a silhouette in the doorway. Her hair was piled loosely on top of her head, the way it always was by the end of a long day. She had a tea towel over her shoulder. I dropped my backpack and fell into her arms. She smelled the way I knew she would, like chocolate chip cookies.

"A dolphin?" she asked skeptically as her arms encircled me. "But Jeni, I've never seen a circus with marine mammals."

"I swear, Mom. It was a dolphin, and a little man was crying over her. There was also a giraffe and a large ape standing by a wrecked truck."

Mom put her hand to my forehead. "You've been driving a long time," she said, leading me into the kitchen. Cooling racks of cookies filled the counters. I grabbed one as she steered me toward the table, savoring every bite as I watched her pile several on a plate and pour two tall glasses of cold milk.

She sat the plate between us on the table.

"Do you need a sandwich? Have you had a good meal?" she asked, her hand hovering near the rim of the plate of cookies as if she were thinking about taking it away.

"Nah, I've eaten. I'm good," I lied.

Mom picked up a cookie and smiled at me. "So tell me about this circus," she sounded amused. I told her everything in detail, from the lights in the distance and my first glimpse of the dolphin and the gypsy girl with no shoes. "A dolphin, a giraffe, an ape," she was ticking off the creatures on her fingers as I finished my story. "This is starting to sound like some sort of Twin Peaks episode," she grinned.

"And a tiger," I said. "Seriously. I didn't see it, but I'm pretty sure I heard a tiger roar."

Chapter 2

I was tempted to stay in bed the next morning, but the smell of biscuits baking in the kitchen was just too much to ignore. I rolled from beneath the covers and surveyed the room, so familiar, yet oddly out of time. My bed was still topped with the blue comforter covered in fluffy clouds that I got for my twelfth birthday. The bulletin board on the wall was covered with perfect attendance and award certificates that dated all the way back to grade school. In the top right corner there were multiple layers of paper for each semester I'd made honor roll in high school.

It was less a bedroom than a shrine to my childhood. Some things I had boxed up and taken with me to college, but much more remained here just where I left it. I imagined my mother stepping into my room, now and then, just to shake the dust off things. It was hard to imagine my mother dwelling in sorrow, but I wondered if she ever just sat on my bed, hugged my old teddy, and just missed me.

I picked him up now and gave him a squeeze. He wasn't soft anymore and the brown fuzz on his nose had been rubbed to bare cloth so long ago that I couldn't actually remember his nose feeling fuzzy, just somehow retained the memory that it once had been so.

The photographs on the mirror were curled with age, that clear "magic" tape still doing its job. I ran my finger along a line of school photos of myself. First grade. Second grade. For some reason third grade was missing. In the fourth grade I'd gotten glasses and in the eighth grade I'd stopped smiling to hide the fact that I was wearing braces. Looking at each photo, I could almost imagine myself again, the person I once was. Closing my eyes made me feel dizzy. It was similar to what I felt when I sat in front of this same mirror as a kid wishing with my whole being to be older, to finally be grown up so that I could get the hell out of Dodge and on with a life that would be more worthwhile and exciting.

Stuck to the bottom right corner of the mirror, nearly hidden by a giant pink jewelry box with a ballet dancer twirling on pointe, was a faded strip from a photo booth. Lisa McKee and I at sixteen. Lisa was my BFF from the third grade—when her family moved in across the street from mine—until our sophomore year when she began dating Tommy Mitchell, the most handsome boy in school. When Lisa started dating Tommy, the bottom fell out of my world. I went from constantly having a friend and companion in everything I did to being completely on my own. Lisa would only make plans with me when Tommy was working or had a school activity that didn't include her. Several times, she'd call me at the last minute, telling me Tommy had suddenly become available and she'd see me next time. When she did manage to make our regular dates, they were always filled with "Tommy this," or "Tommy that." I held out hope that when Tommy went away to Fort Hays the next year, I would get my friend back. It only got worse as Lisa then began spending her days and nights scheming ways to get to Hays to see him.

I'd adjusted, eventually, and found other friends to finish high school with. For several years, though, the very mention of her name brought tears to my eyes. I'd finally gone off to college. She followed Tommy to Hays, but somehow never actually enrolled in school herself. I found my first boyfriend, who was perhaps even more obsessed with birth control than I was, and Lisa got pregnant. She had two kids by the time I graduated from KU. I saw her nearly every time I made it home for a holiday or school break, but the old ease of our friendship was long gone.

The last update Mom gave me about Lisa was that she and Tommy were living with her folks and helping to take care of Lisa's mother, who Mom said was having issues with her memory. She was extremely young to be dealing with dementia, but Mom guessed that something like early Alzheimer's was setting in. The family didn't talk much about it, Mom said, but that was the way the story was being told around town.

I pulled back the faded blue curtains and peered across the street at Lisa's house, the reflection of the morning sun bouncing off its windows. I wondered how many times I'd stood staring out this window waiting for some sign of life from Lisa's place so that we could meet on the street between our houses to start our day. It was odd to think that she was still over there, and me again in my old bedroom. I wondered if she had seen my car. I wondered if she ever thought of me.

My dad and my brother were already at the kitchen table shoveling in Mom's homemade biscuits by the handful. Zach jumped up and gave me a giant bear hug. "Jen-Jen!" he shouted and lifted me from the floor. When he put me down again we high-fived and I knuckle-rubbed his head for old time's sake.

Dad's hug was much more civilized. "Glad to have you home, Baby Girl," he whispered into my hair before kissing me on the forehead. I took my place at the table, noting that Zach and my mother had changed designated seats. Zach was at the foot of the table across from my dad, and Mom took the chair across from me where Zach used to sit.

"So you did see a circus wreck last night," Mom said first thing.

I'd nearly forgotten, or had somehow successfully mixed the visions of last night so far into my dreams that I had not thought of them, for the moment, as real.

"Dude. This circus was passing through," Zach explained, "Acrobats. A bearded lady. An orangutan that plays baseball. Hard core carnival stuff."

"Says here they had camels and giraffes," my Dad said, shaking the morning paper and smoothing its pages on the table in front of him.

"I told you," my brother said with both eyebrows raised, using his whole face to make his point. "They're all in the corral at Kelvin Shepherd's house, just south of town. He and his dad had to help round them up last night. It wasn't even one of the trucks that was wrecked, but the orangutan opened the gate and let two camels and a giraffe loose."

The expression on my mother's face was somewhere between a smirk and disbelief.

"And you were right about the dolphin," Mom said.

Dad read, "A 3,000 gallon aquarium filled the bed of the truck that crossed over the highway dividing line. Witnesses say the sudden shift of the weight of the water caused the aquarium walls to burst, spilling Tabitha the dolphin and seven sea otters into the ditch. As of press time, four of the sea otters had been captured and are in good condition at Stueve's Veterinary Clinic. The dolphin was pronounced dead at the scene."

My brother frowned and then forced a laugh. "Stueve's got otters! I gotta get over there today." Zach worked at the veterinary clinic through the summers. Occasionally he talked about becoming a veterinarian, but usually his career plans were more along the lines of computers and video game design.

"A representative from PETA says that the Menagerie has been on PETA's watch list ever since acquiring the dolphin last summer. The organization has filed multiple injunctions against the menagerie and last protested when the group performed in Harveyville, a small town near Topeka, Kansas where animals were filmed living in cramped and unsuitable quarters.

"A dolphin in Kansas. It just sounds crazy," Mom said.

"Poor dolphin," I sighed, thinking about that sad little man's face as he walked down the road.

"Poor camels. Poor giraffe. Poor orangutan," my brother said.

Mom spread homemade strawberry preserves across a biscuit and passed the spoon to me. I pulled another biscuit from the basket, bringing my total eaten to five. James said my parents have atrocious eating habits and he's probably right, but there is nothing better than Mom's homemade biscuits for breakfast, and they were even better when there was a plate of bacon and some gravy in the mix.

Thinking about James made my throat go dry. I grabbed my brother's glass of orange juice and took a swig to get the last bite of biscuit down.

"Manners much?" Zach scowled at me, clearing his plate from the table. "Hey Jen-Jen, wanna go to school with me today?"

I stuck out my tongue and made a pflttt noise at him. "No. Thank. You," I said.

"It'll be fun. Last day for seniors. You can come watch your little bro be king of the school for the final time."

My brother was six years younger than me, thank goodness. I cringed, thinking of what my life would have been like if we had shared our high school years. Zach was so smooth, so at ease with himself. I'd have been jealous of him if I hadn't been fortunate to be far enough ahead that he really didn't realize just how much of an outcast geek I'd been in high school. The teachers loved me; I'd had that going for me. But I'd never been more than a bench warmer in sports and my artistic eye was only about a fraction of what my brother had. Zach was also smart in math and science and was known for correcting an English teacher or two for poor use of grammar. The girls began flocking all over him starting the day he turned thirteen.

I was awed by my little brother, but had always been careful not to let him know it. When he came to me about matters of intimacy with his girlfriend, I advised him as if my proof-positive information came from actual experience rather than just a book. "If you get a girl pregnant," I'd finished my pep talk, "I will castrate you myself before making sure you stick around to pay child support."

Zach finished rinsing his dishes and put them in the dishwasher. Mom jumped up and took my plate. Zach rolled his eyes. "You really shouldn't treat her like a guest," he said. Mom just winked at me, then gave Zach a peck on the cheek and said, "Now get your butt to school. Can't be late on your last day as king."

I watched the two of them wrestle before leaving the kitchen. Zach and my mom were a lot alike, both bundles of energy, always on the move. I was more like my dad, still and sedate. We were thinkers and puzzlers who were not likely to take action until we'd pondered every course.

Dad was still turning pages of the newspaper, but looking at me with an expectant expression. Eventually he said, "So... the back seat of your car is awfully full. You're not planning on moving back in, are you?"

I looked at the table and found a spot to scrub with my thumb.

Mom had returned to the dishwasher and I could tell she was listening for my response, as well.

Dad looked at his watch. "I'd really like to talk about it now," he said. "But I suppose it can wait till this evening if you are not ready."

Mom came back to the table and sat down across from me. She reached out and took my hands. I didn't want them to see me cry, but too late I realized the tears were already leaking. "That ass," Mom muttered under her breath.

"No, Mom," I managed to say. "It's not like that. It's not his fault."

My parents had never liked James. When my mother figured out my junior year in college that I was dating one of my teachers, she'd blown a gasket. Though I'd assured her, even if it wasn't entirely true, that our relationship hadn't started until the class was over, my mother had never found peace with the matter. When James had come home with me, exactly twice after I'd graduated from KU, my mother greeted him with chilly silence. My father made small talk and had been polite. It was exactly the opposite of the way they would have treated any other boyfriend. My mom was usually the chatty one; my dad the silent observer.

Beyond the initial meltdown, things between my parents and me had gone pretty smoothly. James declined the last few opportunities he had to travel home with me, and when he accepted a position at the University of Houston last year, my parents smiled with gritted teeth and sent me off, making it clear that they would love me always, even if they didn't approve. They'd brought my brother down to visit at Christmas and we had a great time. James had flown to Nebraska to spend the holidays with his own family, whom I have never met.

Zach came rushing down the stairs and yelled farewells to us before bursting out of the house. The blinds on the kitchen windows smacked and rattled from the impact of the front door closing. My mother brought her hand up to her eyes. "Eighteen years and he still doesn't get it," she sighed. "He aced physics, but can't seem to figure out how to move through the house without bringing the walls down."

Dad was focused on the paper again. Mom looked at the clock on the microwave. "What time are you headed in?" she asked.

My father shrugged. "Soon. I'm supposed to be meeting with a rep from Nevada this morning. Some new solar company, supposed to be twice as efficient and half as costly."

My father has run his own construction company since he was twenty. For most of my life, he's put up those big metal buildings. Giant garages for some; businesses for others. But dad has always had these ideas about building and construction. For as long as I can remember I would watch him sketch out plans for buildings that heated and cooled by ways other than the traditional. Now and then he would sell a guy on some plan like putting hot water pipes through the concrete floor as a form of heat, or cooling a big building through an underground shaft that used a fan to draw in cool air. People always seemed to be impressed with his ideas and they mostly always worked, but it was hard getting people to do anything that wasn't the standard way of doing things. My dad says most people are sheep by nature.

In the last ten years or so, however, a lot of my dad's ideas had started catching on. Right after I graduated from high school, he officially changed his business to focus on efficient and alternative building planning and construction. He was doing it before anyone in Kansas knew what LEEDS certification stood for and his income had suffered for it.

Mom told me the last time we talked on the phone that she thought this might be the year Dad's business finally turned around again. When the town of Greensburg was wiped from the map by a tornado and it was decided they would come back all green and truly lean, people started looking at my dad again like maybe he did have something more than rocks in his head.

Mom flipped her wrist and looked at her watch. "I've got private lessons starting at nine until noon," she said. "Are you going to be able to entertain yourself for the morning?"

Mom's job was constantly evolving. When I was a kid, she led aerobics classes and specialized in an exercise called callenetics. She moved to her own version of jazzercise before any of the exercise studios in Wichita were doing it. She's taught adult ballet, tap, and a variety of other dance forms, sometimes learning the moves just barely ahead of her students. When she started offering classes in yoga, the whole town was nearly stood on end. She had students who had taken her classes for years stop showing up because they were afraid she had crossed to the dark side. A couple of local preachers actually visited our house to discuss their concerns with her, the state of her soul, as well as encouraging her to consider the spiritual health of the community.

This only prompted Mom to dig further, of course. At first she was simply interested in yoga as one more form of exercise to add to her ever-growing arsenal that she referred to as movement arts. Then she stopped saying Downward Dog in favor of Adho Mukha Svanasana. She started saying Namaste at the end of each class, as well as in her everyday encounters. And the people of our town began to adapt, as they always do, because Mom was still the person who truly cared about their physical health and helped them to ease their backaches and eliminate their pains.

Mom would tackle anyone's discomfort and work until she'd found a cure that didn't involve drugs or surgery. When Anita Spriggs hurt her back helping her husband butcher a hog, Mom taught her about the importance of remaining flexible and finding physical as well as mental balance. Two years later, Anita told everyone in earshot that, thanks to Mom, she was stronger than she had ever been. Even as a teenager, she had not been so in touch with her body and pleased with her level of fitness.

Mom had a studio out back in a large metal shed that Dad outfitted to meet my mother's every need, and those of her students. She booked a surprising number of private lessons now that a new orthopedic surgeon had moved to town who was totally into the idea of fixing the body naturally if at all possible. He regularly referred patients to Mom and they met on a weekly basis to go over strengthening plans.

"You could come to work with me," Dad said, standing up from the table and stretching his arms slowly into the air. "I'd better hit the shower."

"I'm good," I addressed both of them. "I just want to hang out. Maybe I'll go back to bed for a while."

Mom looked at me the way she often did. I tended to read it as disappointment. I've spent my whole life feeling like she wanted more from me. Mom was so driven, constantly working a plan to improve herself, gain more knowledge, meet a challenge she hadn't yet met. I never wanted quite enough for her. My compass-less existence drove her nuts, at times, but she mostly kept her tongue about it. Above all, it was important to her that I felt loved and supported, something she'd never quite felt she'd gotten enough of from her own parents whom she once described to me as judgmental and critical. I knew it was my mother's greatest goal to be the exact opposite of her own parents.

The crazy thing about both my parents is that they had achieved all their successes without setting foot in a college classroom. Mom tried taking classes when I was in grade school, but grew frustrated because she said she threw herself so deeply into her studies that she would end up knowing more than the teacher. She finally declared herself an autodidactic, a self-teacher, and has never talked about a college degree for herself again. My brother and I, however, grew up knowing that college was a definite part of our future. Zach and I were both encouraged to start taking dual credit classes in high school and my brother, in fact, was only a few hours away from entering college as a sophomore.

I got up from the table and slipped upstairs to escape her gaze. She was, in fact, a very outwardly supportive mother, and I was willing to admit I probably spent more time trying to read her between the lines than was healthy. Aside from the fit she had thrown about my relationship with James, I can't remember her ever really having issues with the way I chose to live my life. She avoided offering advice unless I specifically asked, and even then she tended to do more questioning than asking, forcing me to pull the answers from within myself. Sometimes I wished she had spent more time telling me what to do. I found it pretty easy to follow orders. That's how I'd gotten through high school and college. Whatever my instructors suggested, I was willing to comply. In the two years since I finished college, I can't say I'd done anything productive or worthwhile, and my job didn't even require a college diploma. I moved boxes around a warehouse. My parents thought I actually worked in retail sales. I'd never had the heart to tell them I couldn't face dealing with customers every day. The warehouse job gave me lots of time to spend inside my head, which was honestly what I did best. James always told me I should be writing novels. It's what I think I'm doing, inside my head, but any attempt I've ever made to write them down on paper leaves me disappointed. I don't seem to have the skill to translate my stories into word form that can be printed in a book.

    I slipped into my childhood bedroom and piled the pillows up at the end of the small bed so that I could watch out the window. Big balls of white fluff dotted the blue sky. I curled up in the stack of pillows and pulled teddy to me, tucking him under my arm the way I did when I was a kid. I let my eyes travel up and down the street until the door of Lisa's house opened. I watched my childhood friend kiss her handsome husband and shuttle three small and lovely children to a green minivan parked in their driveway. Lisa was talking animatedly and the oldest of the kids was singing a silly song I almost recognized. I hummed the tune under my breath, unable to come up with the words.

    Lisa suddenly stopped talking and looked around. It was as if she could feel me studying her. She looked at our house, seemed to take in the details of my car parked in the driveway, then shaded her eyes and looked up to my window. The blinds were open just enough so I could see out. Between that and the sun climbing over our house in the sky, I didn't think she could see me. Her face remained blank. She finally turned her attention back on her kids and climbed into the minivan. The brake lights flickered, then the reverse, and I watched her drive away. I leaned back on my pillows, ready to lose myself in a story, thinking maybe this one would be the one, finally, that I could turn into words on paper.

    Her sudden braking caught my attention, however, and I leaned forward to look out the window again. There was a small brown creature in the street. I saw Lisa hang her head out the window, straining to see it clearly.

    Her eyes weren't deceiving her. An otter was slinking alongside the curb.

Chapter 3

I opened my eyes later to see Mom standing in the doorway. She looked toward the window and smiled. "I can't tell you how many times I've walked into this room to find you curled up at the foot of your bed, staring out this window. I never understood why you wouldn't just turn the bed around and sleep with your head at this end to start with."

I smiled, an attempt to act as if I wasn't sleeping deeply. I stifled a yawn. "I liked the view from the corner too," I said.

"You hungry? I'm done with clients for the day. I thought maybe we could go out to eat, just you and I."

"Sure. Jalisco's?"

She nodded. Jalisco's was this tiny little Mexican restaurant that my mom and I had started frequenting my senior year in high school. It was an orange and yellow building, so brightly painted it took the gringos a couple of years before they started setting foot in the place with frequency. Good food is hard to resist, however. The food was so good and the place so frequently packed that last year they razed the restaurant and built a new one, a metal building like my dad used to build. It's a town favorite now, and just like my Mom's yoga studio, it is constantly filled with all walks and talks.

"This diversity is good for a town like ours," Mom always said, and Jalisco's clientele is about as multicultural as it gets. The food is straight Mexico, however. They serve their meals on tiny corn tortillas. Even living in Houston, which has some of the best Tex-Mex restaurants in the world, I would find myself longing for a Jalisco's taco plate.

I practically jumped from the bed and pulled my shoes on. I pulled my wallet from my backpack while Mom disappeared down the hall into her bedroom. I grabbed my cell phone and checked for messages. Nothing.

Mom was quick, she was watching me from the doorway again by the time I looked up.

"Are you expecting to hear from him?" she asked.

"Nah. Not really," I answered, shrugging the question off like it was no big deal. James knew I was headed to Kansas for my brother's high school graduation and I wasn't entirely sure he would have realized by now, just how gone I was. I'd packed my giant backpack, the one I'd bought my senior year in college while planning some crazy trip backpacking in Europe with a girl I'd had several English classes with. We hadn't gone. I'd moved in with James, instead, and for a little while James seemed worth giving up the trip.

The twelve hour drive home had given me plenty of time to run the story through my head. I pictured James arriving at the house we shared, walking through the door with his brief case under his arm the way he always carried it, instead of using the handle. He'd paw through the mail on the table and then shove it to the center where it would join the heap that James always let pile up. I wondered if he would think to pull the important items, like the bills, and put them in the bill box. The box was my designation, of course, as was the desk where all the bill paying happened. James had the beautiful oak roll top when I met him and, as far as I could tell, it was nothing more than decoration for him. At some point, he would notice that my lamp was gone, the tiny Queen Ann lamp with the blue lily of the valleys painted on the glass shade. He'd get up and wander into the living room, noting that my bookshelf was empty. Of the hundreds of books in the room, he'd notice the three foot space where my collection resided.

Furrowing his brow in that way he always did when feeling overlooked by his administrators or underappreciated by his students, he'd move quickly to the bedroom where he'd see that I'd taken my pillow and stripped the bed of its spread. It was one of the few things I'd added to James's household, one of the few things that wasn't tucked into a closet or left sitting in a box in a storage room. I'd selected and purchased the comforter that covered the bed, and though I honestly couldn't see myself sleeping under it again, I didn't want James to sleep under it either.

"I drive. You talk," Mom said, locking the door and wiggling the handle hard to assure herself it was secure.

I climbed into the passenger seat of her car. I glanced at my car as she backed past it and into the road. In the daylight, it was conspicuously full. There was no way to claim that this was just a visit, or that I was simply cleaning out some items in hopes of storing them at home. "I'm 24 years old," I said, "And all my earthly belongings still fit into the back seat and trunk of my car."

Mom smiled and I saw her mouth move. She closed it again. "I'm driving," she finally said. "You're talking."

I sighed. I knew I could tell my mother anything without further disappointing her. She had once told me that though she might not be pleased with my actions, there was nothing in the world that I could ever do that would stop her from loving me without condition. I decided to start at the beginning.

"The first time I was with James..." I almost threw a date in there, but caught myself. I could start at the beginning without admitting that I'd begun seeing James while I was still his student. "There was another woman's shoes under the bed. There were birth control pills in the medicine cabinet, and a woman's razor, shampoo, and bath soaps in the shower."

Mom bit her lip, but kept driving in silence.

"I'm just saying that I knew this about him when I met him. I knew this, and I should have known better. You taught me better than this."

Mom's eyes flicked in my direction, but she just kept driving.

"He's been coming home later and later. Often he misses supper altogether. It's the only time we really have to spend together. I work at night, and he's at the university all day. At first he would call, make excuses and all that, but more and more he just doesn't show up. He stays gone until past the time I have to leave for work and on weekends he's busy with this project or that."

Mom cleared her throat, but otherwise stayed silent behind the wheel.

"Last week there was a hairbrush in the bathroom. Not mine. Not his. It had long blond hair in it." I sighed. Laying this out for my mother felt something like confession. I was a bit embarrassed, but also relieved.

"I'm so dense. I knew this about James. I knew when I started seeing him that there was another woman living in his house. Yet I'd just kept seeing him. And here I am now, the woman whose shoes are still under the bed. I'm there, and he's moved on. Just like I always knew he would, I guess."

Mom had both lips pulled into her mouth in a tight crease. Her checks were indented and I could see the strain on her brow. Keeping quiet wasn't easy for her and I loved her all the more for the effort she was making.

"I'm 24 years old," I said again, "And all my earthly belongings still fit into the back seat and trunk of my car."

Mom had turned into the parking lot of Jalisco's. She put the car in park and reached across, putting her warm hand over mine on my lap. She chewed at her lip. I wondered if her head might actually explode if I went on like this, talking just enough to reinforce her promise to herself to remain silent. I imagined the words she was swallowing.

"It's okay Mom. You can call him all the names you'd like now. It really isn't going to bother me." I smiled to show her just how okay I was.

It took a moment for her expression to change, "Well then," she said, and started grinning, but her face quickly grew serious again. She pressed her lips back into that thin line that I always associated with words unsaid.

"Sometimes," she finally said. "Sometimes the best thing is to just keep moving forward." She patted my hand gently. "You know that you are always welcome here, and if you need a place to stay for a while, your room is still your room."

I couldn't help but think my mother had expected this all along. My friends, their parents had cleaned out their bedrooms as quickly as possible, turned them into guest rooms, exercise rooms, or offices. My room remained mine. I'd always felt that she left it intentionally, as if she understood that I wasn't done needing it.

"What I want you to think about," Mom was still speaking seriously, "Is if coming back here, moving into your old room, will prevent you from moving forward."

I swallowed. These words were unexpected. "It'd just be temporary," I stuttered. "I'm not going to move back forever, just for a little while. Maybe a few weeks."

Mom nodded and patted my hand some more, then bit her lower lip again, swallowing more words, before opening the car door and stepping out into the bright blue day. The wind whipped the ruffles on her blouse and blew her short wavy hair into straight lines standing out from her head. She reached up her hand to smooth it and turned to look at me over the car as I held my door fast to keep it from being ripped from my hands in the sudden gust.

"Welcome home, Baby," she shouted at me over the wind.

I grinned. There was nothing like a good western Kansas breeze to clear the head.

We stood in line at the counter, waiting to place our order and pay. I'd grabbed a colorful take-home menu even though I knew I was going to order my standard taco meal platter.

"Jeni? Jeni Renzelmen?"

I heard the high pitched voice and was immediately taken back to high school. I turned to see Carlie Eckles, still wearing her high school letter jacket, waving and headed my direction.

"Hi, Carlie," I said in a voice so low I doubted she heard me.

"I knew that was you the minute you walked in the door!" Carlie hugged me. I was more than a little taken aback. Carlie and I had gone to the same grade school. We were once close, exchanging overnights and taking turns "going with" the same boy through most of the fourth grade. But Carlie had become a cheerleader in high school and, though we weren't enemies or anything, we'd probably said all of a half dozen words to each other through our last six years in school together. In short, Carlie was popular and I tended to drift on the fringes of the crowds who really didn't think a whole lot of girls who were cheerleaders.

"Mrs. Renzelmen!" Carlie hugged my Mom, too. "Did your mom tell you, Jeni?" she turned her attention back to me, "I'm taking classes at your mom's studio and she's training me to fill in for her so she can take some time off."

I looked at my mom, confused. "No," I shook my head. "Really?" I asked Mom.

It seemed like something she maybe ought to have mentioned, that my old friend was being trained as her replacement. I felt a twinge of jealously.

Mom just smiled and patted Carlie on the shoulder. "It'll be nice having an evening off now and then," she said. "I've been teaching at least three movement classes a day for almost twenty years now."

"And did you hear?" Carlie was looking back and forth between us. "About the circus? The wreck last night? Those poooooor animals. That pooooor dolphin." Each time she said the word poor, the pitch of her voice went up and down and then up again. Carlie often had the lead in the school dramas, both on stage and off.

"I saw..." I started to say, but Carlie cut me off.

"They still haven't found the tiger! A white tiger, can you imagine? Running loose in western Kansas!"

It was our turn at the counter. Mom ordered for me. She's usually a more adventurous eater than I am, but she agreed that the taco platter was equivalent to the best food ever.

"Coronas?" Mom asked. "Is it too early in the day for a beer?" She looked to Carlie, who looked back rather puzzled and shrugged her shoulders.

"You drink beer, Mrs. Renzelman? I never pictured you a beer drinker."

My Mom smiled at Carlie and winked at me. "Everything in moderation, Carlie. That's my motto."

Three classes a day for twenty years, I thought. Yeah, that sounded like moderation.

Carlie had come from a table full of people, but followed us to ours after we ordered. She was chatting away about some yoga workshop she and my mother were scheduled to go to in Wichita this summer. Mom and I stared across the table at each other. I lifted my eyebrows, hoping Mom would take it as a cue to give Carlie the shoo-fly treatment.

She did.

"Carlie, Jeni and I have some catching up to do. Let's you and I talk more about the studio plans tomorrow after class, okay?"

Carlie caught right on. She hugged me again and hugged Mom. "It's so good to see you, Jeni. I keep up with you through your Mom, but it sure is nice seeing you in person."

My mother knew full well that Carlie had more or less dumped me once we'd graduated from the sixth grade, and apparently she and Mom were on plenty enough good terms without Carlie having to make up with me. I just nodded in response, smiled as sincerely as I could muster, and watched Carlie bounce back to the table she had come from.

"A white tiger," I said, trying to imagine what was newsworthy enough about me for Mom to have spent any time talking to Carlie about me at all. She was probably just being nice. "I told you I heard a tiger roar last night when I was driving by. I saw the ape and then I heard a roar. It was a big cat roar. I'm sure of it."

"Hmm," Mom made her thoughtful sound. "I've heard so many rumors about that circus today. That the ape was actually the one driving. That the ape was riding in the passenger seat and attacked the driver. That someone had sabotaged the vehicle—probably one of those PETA people—or possible the ape—when it was stopped at the truck stop out south of town. There's no telling what is truth and what is fiction."

"I did hear a roar. I'm certain it was a big cat now that I think about it."

I thought about Lisa this morning and the otter. She'd stopped her van in the street and run across the yard, back into her house. She'd come out with her father, who had opened the garage door and disappeared inside for a few minutes. Lisa sat out on the curb offering apple slices to the alien beastie. It had come right to her. It was obviously tame. While Lisa had been feeding the otter, waiting for her dad to come out of the garage with a big giant net and a cardboard box he apparently thought was appropriate for capturing it, she'd looked up toward my window a couple of times, as if she could feel me watching her. I'd kept visualizing myself going outside, walking across the yard and saying hey to her, just like I'd done a million times as we were growing up. I could picture it happening a dozen different ways, but never moved from my bed.

She and her dad got the thing into the box. The otter seemed to think it was a game. It kept going in and out, begging for another apple slice, then rolling summersaults and diving into the box again. Lisa and her dad were both laughing by the time they got the box flaps closed tight. Lisa held them down, poking the otter's nose down each time it appeared, while her dad went back into the garage to get a board to keep the otter from getting out. She then pulled her cell phone out of her pocket and called someone. I figured she was calling Stueve's Vet Clinic. She surely would have heard that the other otters were being housed there, as well.

Both Lisa and Carlie had once been my good friends. I lost Carlie to high school cliques and Lisa to a boy. I wondered how it was that I'd ended up in my twenties with no real girlfriends. No real friends at all, come to think about it, considering I'd given the last three years of my time and attention to a man who was apparently able to move on without so much as a thought about my feelings in the matter.

Mom carefully squeezed a lime into her beer and then stuffed the wedge into the bottle. We watched the golden liquid foam up when the citric acid hit the drink. Mom took a swig. She leaned back in the booth. I tried to mimic her posture. My mother always exuded confidence. Home or away, she always seemed at ease with her surroundings. And people were drawn to her. She'd been waved at by at least a half dozen people just since we'd been in the restaurant, not including Carlie.

"So," she said. "You've loaded all of your earthly belongings into your car. You didn't tell the man you've been living with that you weren't intending to return. Job? Did you quit your job? Take a sabbatical?"

"I... kind of quit," I said guiltily.

"Two weeks' notice. I'm sure you gave them proper notice to fill your spot?"

I grabbed a lime from the bowl and began milking it into my own Corona. "I'm not exactly irreplaceable," I said.

Mom's eyebrows were high on her forehead. Then she seemed to have some sort of inner dialogue with herself and her face relaxed. She took on more of a soft expression. I knew she was working me, working herself so that I would open up and keep talking.

"I told a co-worker," I admitted. "He passed on the message that I wouldn't be coming back."

Mom had her elbows on the table. She squeezed her hands together rapidly a few times, looked away, took a barely perceptible, slow and deep breath, and then looked at me again, smiling. She was going to let this pass without a lecture. I was 24 years old after all. I pictured her telling my dad that she was going to stop lecturing me. I could somehow imagine exactly how the conversation went.

Sometimes I felt as if I knew more about what went on between people when I wasn't around than when I was. An overactive imagination, I suppose. I'd been accused all through grade school of being a day dreamer. I'd learned to apply myself, when necessary, and got through high school with less of a reputation for lollygagging. But I'd never stopped reading between the lines of every conversation. I'd never stopped thinking about what was going on inside the head of every person I'd met, creating elaborate stories and events full of detail.

I watched people. I taught myself to understand their body language. I could watch two people from across a room and come away understanding how they felt about each other, but I was a lousy conversationalist.

"Let's just suppose that James gives you a call. Let's say he does realize you're gone and he's upset about it."

Mom was testing me.

"I suppose I'll just jump in the car and drive right back to Houston," I said.

Tiger Hunting

Mom's eyebrows fell into a deep V on her forehead.

I shook my head, attempting a lighthearted grin at her. "Mom, really. I know. You told me from the start. James isn't the guy for me. He never was. I don't know why… it was just, he was so easy to follow."

"Follow," Mom repeated. She rested her head on her hand and shook her head slightly. Her face registered pain and it pained me that I could hurt her so. The waitress arrived at our table with the food. We both looked at the plates gratefully, lowered our heads and started eating.

I paused a moment to take a long drink of the beer. Mom looked up at me and smiled. She grabbed hers and we clinked them together.

"Here's to moving forward," she said.

"Moving forward," I said. "Forward without following."

And this brought the biggest, most sincere smile to my mother's face that I had seen since I arrived.

Chapter 4

My cell phone jingled as we walked back out to the car, the sign that a text message had been received. I pulled it out of my pocket and flipped it open.

It read:

department party Saturday. might u b home? dean says she misses u. wants you there 4 big announcement. xoxo ME

James always signed his name ME when he was emailing or texting me. It once was one of his many qualities I found endearing.

"Everything okay?" Mom asked.

"Um..." I deleted the message and slammed my cell phone shut. "Yeah, it's all good." I put on my brightest smile and looked at her. Her quick smile back made me assume that she bought it.

I turned toward the window and gritted my teeth. That jerk didn't even understand that I had left him. I packed all my earthly belongings and left a note on the table. A very crowded and cluttered table, admittedly, but still. How on earth could he miss that I was gone?

Zach burst through the door at exactly 3:15 and ran up the stairs, shouting, "Get your shoes on Jen-Jen! We're going hunting!"

Mom and I were stacking the final boxes from my car into my closet.

"You want to go, Mom? We're hunting white tiger," he shouted as he stuck his head into my room.

"You are not!" I shouted, following Zach down the hall and into his room. He was digging through the bottom of his closet. "You can't hunt that poor animal!"

"Not hunting like bang-bang," Zach laughed at me. "Doc Stueve's got tranquilizer guns. Can't let an animal like that run loose in Kansas. Get your shoes on. I told him I'd bring along the best shot in western Kansas."

I had been a pretty good shot as a 4-Her in shooting sports. I had no desire—ever—to hunt, and I'd actually become a something like a vegetarian since living with James. He wouldn't allow meat in his kitchen, so it wasn't like I had a whole lot of choice. Zach was ten when I'd won the county, then district, then state competition with a rifle. Dad drove us to Kentucky for the national competition. I'd ending up placing 7th in the nation. Lucky shot after lucky shot, I always supposed.

I hadn't picked up a gun since. I'd spent one more year in 4-H, then graduated high school and went to college at KU, a place that wasn't full of many with an aptitude or attitude for guns. Most of my friends had gone to K-State, the agricultural college. I can't exactly say why I chose one over the other, except that maybe I was slightly more partial to the color blue than the color purple.

Mom came into Zach's room. "There really is a missing tiger?" she asked.

"Yep. Stueve's been out looking all day with some midget from the circus and a bearded lady, who also happens to be the cat trainer," Zach said.

"It's like we're living in a Twin Peaks episode," my mother said, shaking her head.

"You coming Jen-Jen?" Zach had fished a knapsack off the bottom of his closet floor and was stuffing his digital camera and about a dozen batteries inside. "You shoot the tranquilizer gun for Doc Stueve and I'll document the whole thing on camera."

He grinned at us. His hair was tousled and he looked about twelve. I fought an urge to throw my arms around him, squeeze him tight and give him another knuckle rub across the top of his head.

"Sure," I said with a shrug. "I don't have much else planned this afternoon."

Zach bounded out of his bedroom and hit maybe four steps of the stairs on his way down. I rushed to follow him, glancing quickly back at my mom who was standing at the top of the stairs, leaning against Zach's doorway with her arms crossed over her chest. She was grinning from ear to ear.

Zach barely waited for me to get the door of his little red pickup truck closed. "We's hunting tiger," he said, throwing the truck into drive and leaving black marks on the street in front of our house as he gunned it.

There were a lot of pickup trucks at Doc Stueve's Clinic when we arrived. I glanced around, expecting to see at least a couple of people that I knew, and I did. A couple of Zach's best friends and classmates high-fived me. Doc Stueve lifted his chin and gave me a wink when I followed Zach into the clinic. "So he did bring you along," Stueve said. "Still got your aim girl?"

I shrugged my shoulders, accepting the tranquilizer gun Doc passed across the counter at me. "It's been a few years, Doc. I can't promise you anything."

"I got six guns," Doc said. "Called every veterinarian in the county to round these up, plus the two that the circus folk had. One of these darts should take down a full grown tigress. She ain't really dangerous, I hope. Hand-raised since she was a kit, but she's a big animal and wild is in her nature. We don't know what happened when those trucks overturned. She could be hurt. She's probably scared. And we just aren't taking any chances.

"They've left the circus truck open in the field out there all day, hoping she'd just return to it, but nobody's seen a thing. The guys at the airport took up a plane at noon today, hoping to give us a spot. We think she went southwest, according to the footprints, but with a road every square mile it's hard telling what kind of course she might be following. Probably looking for water. I expect we'll hear from a farmer sooner or later that they've found her at a stock pond or tank, or worse, that she's taken down a calf. Don't know if this one will hunt just yet, but the longer she's out there, the more likely that she will try."

Doc was breathless and almost as giddy as my kid brother.

"You gotta come see this Jen-Jen," my brother said. He slipped around behind Doc's counter and led me through a doorway to the back. We went through the room full of dog kennels and looked in through the window of a larger building outback. Inside was a big cattle stock tank full of water. Five brown otters were tossing a red ball around, sloshing water over the side. "Cute, don't ya think?"

Zach opened the door just enough for the two of us to slip inside. The otters all paused for a moment, looking in our direction. One dove under the water entirely and started racing in circles at the bottom of the tank. Two came forward and over the side, rushing toward us, their little bodies slinking like slinkies. Zach took something from a bag on the wall and kneeled down. The otters were all over him, through and around his legs, begging for more treats.

"How did you..." I started to ask.

Zach grinned. "Hell. I left school just after lunch today. What was they going to do? Kick me out?"

"So you've been here all afternoon playing with otters?" I asked. "Why didn't you come get me sooner?"

"Not just otters," Zach said. "Come look at this."

He grabbed a handful of treats and headed toward the door. When we got there, he turned and threw the treats a little ways back toward the stock tank, the otters that were following, three of them now, zipped back to catch what he had thrown and while they were distracted, we quickly squeezed ourselves through the door.

I followed Zach around back to the corrals where Doc kept cattle, horses, or whatever large animals he happened to be treating at any point in time. I'd seen llamas out there a few times, but seeing a giraffe standing there took my breath away. She was so tall I wondered how easy it would be for her to just walk right over the bars intended for far shorter animals.

"We put up two lines of electric wire this afternoon," Zach said as if he was reading my mind. "She hasn't really tested them, but Doc figured we were better safe than sorry. There were two camels in the next pen over and a gorgeous silver horse with braids and bows in its mane in the far pen. All of the animals moved to the front of the pens and looked at us expectantly.

"Where are the circus people? Why are they just leaving the animals here?" I asked.

Zach shrugged. "Don't know. That story is getting weirder and weirder. Drunken clowns and midgets and bearded ladies – more than an act for most of these folks."

"The orangutan?" I asked.

Zach turned toward me and grinned. "Orville. You've got to meet Orville."

I followed him back into the clinic. Doc Stueve's waiting room was getting full of boys dressed like cowboys and cowboys dressed like truckers. Doc was telling the group about the tigress and the plane that had gone up this afternoon to no avail. I followed Zach down the hallway to Doc's office. A large, red-haired orangutan was sitting at Doc's desk, staring at the telephone like he was expecting it to ring.

Zach knocked twice on the door and the ape looked up. It pursed its lips at Zach and then grinned, showing all its teeth. Zach loped on in. I stayed by the door. The ape stared at me for a moment before putting its feet down to the floor and slowly walking around the desk. It moved like a little old man. Walked right up to me and pursed its lips, sticking its face right up close to mine.

"Orville, this is my sister, Jeni," Zach said. "Jen-Jen, this is Orville, and I believe he's asking for a kiss."

I turned my face away, afraid the beast might actually try to plant one on me. I put my hand out. "Nice to meet you, Orville," I said.

The ape took my hand and held it like a lost little boy. The top of his head came to about my nose. He leaned over, putting his head on my shoulder. I was nearly paralyzed with fright. I kept trying to reassure myself that Doc Stueve wouldn't just let this animal run loose in his office if it wasn't trustworthy.

"Zach! Jeni!" Doc was calling from the front office. "We're heading out."

"Gotta go, Orville," Zach said. The ape followed us out of Doc's office. There was a very short little man standing beside the Doc and a rather stocky individual whom I supposed might be the bearded lady, but she was clean shaven. Orville grabbed my hand and pulled me, grabbing the hand of the woman, as well, and standing between us like he was ready to go somewhere. The circus woman didn't even look at me. She seemed to be staring at some spot on the ceiling. She reached out absentmindedly with her free hand and stroked Orville's head. The ape leaned toward her, puckering his lips and kissing her on the side of the face.

I tried to excuse myself politely, but the ape held tight. I looked to Zach for help, but Zach was busy handing out hand-held radios to those who were going on the tiger hunt while Doc was assigning each pair a road and a direction. Doc Stueve's receptionist put down the phone. "Mike from the airport will be back up the plane in half an hour. He'll stay in touch with Doc by radio."

I was trying to imagine what direction I might head were I a tiger loose in western Kansas. Unfortunately, my ability to perceive thoughts and motivations didn't extend to tigresses, at least a not to a tigress I had never met. My hand was getting sweaty, holding on to that ape, so I relaxed my fingers and tried to pull away. The ape pulled back, so I pulled harder.

Orville wouldn't look at me, but seemed determined to keep me by his side. I relaxed my hand again and then yanked quickly, thinking I'd trick him into letting go. Orville pulled back so hard and so fast I smacked into him, knocking the bearded lady off balance, as well. We made such a ruckus, Doc Stueve stopped giving direction.

"Let go of me, Orville. Please," I heard myself whimper to an entirely silent room. I looked up to see about a dozen faces staring at me, including that of Joe Stimpert. Joe stepped forward and Orville quickly let go of my hand, holding his hands up as if he were a criminal Joe was threatening to arrest.

"Hey, Jeni," Joe said, his voice a little deeper than I remembered it, his blue eyes just as piercing as they always had been. "How you doing? It's been a long time."

My mouth grew dry. "Hey, Joe," was about all I could manage.

Orville crossed his arms across his chest and shuffled up real close to Joe. The ape puckered his lips and gave Joe a kiss right on the smacker. Joe flinched, jumping backward and wiping at his mouth with the tail of his t-shirt, revealing the fine definition of his abs to anyone who was looking. I couldn't be sure who that might be, because I couldn't seem to take my eyes off Joe. Orville took Joe's hand, blew a raspberry to the air, and showed all his ape teeth in a cheesy grin. Orville batted his eyes and shuffled sideways into Joe, putting his orange head against Joe's shoulder with a big sigh.

Joe was well distracted. Without another thought, I took the opportunity to grab the gun Doc Stueve had designated for me and rushed out the door.

"I'll be waiting in your truck," I whisper-shouted to Zach as I rushed past.

Chapter 5

In spite of my efforts to avoid my junior high crush, I found myself riding in the back of my brother's little red truck with Joe Stimpert and Orville the Orangutan. The bearded lady rode shotgun. My brother seemed to be hitting every bump along the way. I could have sworn he was swerving back and forth to take turns hitting the deepest ruts with his left tire and then his right.

Joe stood braced against the cab, binoculars to his eyes. I tried hard to watch for any sign of a white tiger, but kept finding myself focused, instead, on Joe's blue-jean clad tush. Orville seemed tuned in to my distraction. The ape couldn't seem to keep his eyes off of Joe either. At one point, Orville covered my eyes with his hairy orange hand and grunted at me, making it clear that he had no interest in sharing Joe's affections.

The land was flat. It was hard to imagine that a tiger could hide for long on land like this. We'd been driving the pastures of every farm in Ford and Clark County for a couple of hours. A donkey had chased Zach's truck at one farm and Orville had gotten all excited, standing and making true monkey-type noises for the first time since I'd met him. The ape tried really hard to keep himself between the donkey and Joe. At one point, he reached down and pulled on my hair as if he was considering throwing me out as bait.

The bearded lady had stuck her head out the window, chattered madly for about a minute until Orville acknowledged the scolding. The ape had sat back down, sulking. It still sat with its head down, every now and then reaching up and touching Joe's pant leg.

"I'm not sure this was a good idea," Joe said to me, gesturing toward Orville. "What do we know about chimps anyway?"

Orville stuck out his tongue at Joe. "I don't think he likes being called a chimp. He's an orangutan," I said.

At the fence, Joe leapt out of the truck bed to release the gate. He pulled it open while Zach drove through and we waited while Joe relatched it. Orville and I sighed in unison.

"How did I do it?" I asked the ape. "How did I start with someone like Joe Stimpert and end up with a loser college prof like James?"

Orville patted my leg and looked at me skeptically.

"You're right. It's not like he was ever actually my boyfriend," I said. "But he could have been. Maybe."

The damned ape rolled his eyes at me.

"Oh, and I suppose you think you have a chance with him?"

Orville grinned and lifted his chin. Joe was back at the truck.

"You talking to that ape?" he asked.

"We might be having a bit of a discussion," I answered, giving Orville a slight jab with my elbow. Orville jabbed back, nearly knocking me through the side of the truck bed.

"Ouch," I yelled.

"Hey!" Joe shouted, leaping back into the bed of the truck. "You just calm down now, mister. There's no need to be that way."

The bearded lady was out of the truck in a second. "Don't push Orville," she said to me. "He'll push you right back, and he's an ape. You can't compete with that."

I just looked at her, speechless.

"He shoved her. He could have really hurt her," Joe said, indignant.

Orville blew raspberries and kisses at Joe. Zach got out of the truck.

"Everything okay back here?" he asked.

"I think that ape should be sedated," Joe answered.

The bearded lady threw herself into the back of the truck with surprising speed and agility. "You touch that ape and you'll find yourself sedated," she said, her voice cracking and going whispery.

"He shoved her," Joe said, keeping his tone even.

"She shoved him first," the bearded lady said.

Joe and Zach were both looking at me. Orville bumped me lightly with his elbow, as if to demonstrate.

"I tapped him a bit," I admitted. "He was leaning. I might have pushed him a bit with my elbow to get some space."

The bearded lady looked at Joe and raised her eyebrows as if to say, "See?"

My brother mumbled something under his breath. "Jen-Jen, for god's sake, keep peace with the ape."

"I'm sorry," I said, looking from Zach to Joe to the bearded lady.

Orville hugged his arms tight across his chest and looked down, sticking out his lower lip.

"Oh sheesh," I said. Then finally, "Orville, I'm sorry. I shouldn't have jabbed at you. I'm sorry."

The big ape grinned at me and puckered his lips. I accepted his kiss on my cheek and even refrained from wiping it away, at least until I knew he was looking elsewhere.

"Maybe it's time to call it a day, anyway," Zach said. "We're more than an hour from Dodge City. It's getting dark. And I'm hungry."

I was feeling a bit hungry too, now that my brother brought it up. "Yeah," I agreed. "Let's head home."

But Orville and the bearded lady were gazing off into the sunset. The sky was filling with reds and oranges and yellows.

"God's canvas," my brother said with reverence.

"Amen," said Joe.

We all stood there watching as the fiery ball of the sun fell beneath the horizon. That's when we heard the tiger's roar.

The hair on my arms was standing straight up. The bearded lady jumped from the bed of the truck, moving first toward the setting sun, then away from it. "Which direction did it come from?" she finally asked.

I wasn't sure. I only knew that it was a wild sound, the kind that your body instinctively reacted to before your mind had time to interpret what you were hearing. Zach and Joe and I stood, motionless, waiting to see if the tigress would meow again.

"Here kit-ty kit-ty kit-ty," Joe called out softly.

"Shush!" the bearded lady scolded him. "You sit. Wait here. She'll come to me. She knows me."

I was holding the rifle with the tranquilizer dart at the ready. I must have picked it up without realizing it when I heard that haunting sound.

"You put that down," the bearded lady scolded me. "We don't need that. The tigress knows me. She will come."

I settled my rear against the cab of the truck, bringing the butt of the rifle down from my shoulder, but not entirely relaxing it. Zach jumped back up in the bed of the truck and stood on one side of me. Joe stood on the other. Orville sat down and leaned against the tailgate. The ape began picking at his teeth as if he were bored with it all.

The bearded lady was moving away from the truck in a wide curving path, first going from west to south, then south to west and back again. Now that the sun had set, darkness was coming quickly. I kept my eyes trained on the lady, my ears straining to hear another sound from the tiger. I glanced quickly to my right and left. Zach and Joe seemed to be absorbed in the same event – watching and listening, watching and listening.

Zach got quietly out of the bed of the truck and opened the door to the cab. I heard static from the hand-held radio. "Doc. We've heard her. We heard the tigress, but we haven't seen her yet," I could hear him whisper. He gave Doc directions and then brought the radio back with him into the bed of the truck. Orville was full out lying on his back by this time, looking up at the sky with wide, clear eyes. We three stood there, watching the darkness for sign of the white tiger or the bearded lady and listening for them too.

I could feel the tension drain away from both Zach and Joe on each side of me, as the roar of that tigress faded into memory. Zach finally changed position, leaning against the cab and crossing one foot over the other. Finally, he sat and leaned his head back against the cab, eyes drifting to the stars above. Joe and I remained standing. I realized our breaths were synchronized and I became aware of just how close we were standing. As the temperature of the night air dropped, I could still feel his body heat.

The first vehicles began to arrive from the search party. Doc had dismissed most of the crew for the night, but he and a handful of others had arrived to help us keep watch through the night.

"Where is she?" Doc asked.

I wasn't sure if he was asking about the tigress or the bearded lady. Zach did all the reporting, pointing in the general direction we had last seen the bearded lady. Zach got in the Doc's jeep and they began driving in that direction. A small crowd of us watched as the space lit by the headlights grew smaller.

The other searchers who had arrived with Doc were milling about. One climbed into the back of a Suburban, looking like he might just bed down for the night.

"You really heard her roar?" one asked us from the pickup bed next to ours.

"Sure did," Joe said, and sat down, finally, causing Orville to sit up. The ape scooted a bit and lay back down with his head on Joe's lap.

"This is so weird," Joe said. "Surreal. This orangutan here. A white tiger roaming the fields of western Kansas."

I sat down, too.

"Being here with you, of all people," Joe said.

"Me?" I said, feeling clueless.

"You know. First..." his voice trailed off.

"First what?" I said. First girl who ever stalked him, I was thinking.

"Crush, I guess." He turned and looked at me. "You were the first girl I ever had it really bad for. Seventh grade. Home economics class. You and me and Lisa McKee and Sammi What's-Her-Name."

"Stevens," I filled in for him. "Sammi Stevens was our in our kitchen group in home economics class."

"Yeah, Stevens. That's her."

"You had a crush on me?" I felt tongue-tied, but somehow the words came out okay.

"Oh my god yes," he said, shaking his head like he was a little bit embarrassed. He clutched his chest. "And you barely knew I existed."

"No," I laughed, shaking my head.

"No?" he asked, trying to act offended at me laughing at him.

"It was you who barely noticed me... at least," I was feeling this mixed up swirling of butterflies in my stomach, like my 13-year-old girl self had surfaced again and had just been told, "Joe Stimpert knows who you are!"

"You really had a crush on me?" I asked softly.

Orville rolled over and shoved at my foot, as if trying to put some distance between Joe and myself. He reached up with his long ape arm and started stroking Joe's hair.

"Why didn't you ever say anything?"

"Well..." he seemed to be seriously pondering this. "Aside from juvenile incompetence and general inability to speak whenever you were near... actually, I really thought I did."

"You told me that you liked me?"

"Not in so many words, but yes. I did."

"And what was my response?"

"Well, in the seventh grade you mostly just glared at me. I mean, pretty much every time I talked to you, I kind of felt like you were glaring at me. And then I tried to ask you to the winter homecoming dance when we were in eighth grade, but you ran off before I got the words out. I kind of took it as a no."

"You never... I never... oh my god, I always thought you must have thought of me as a complete idiot. I was always staring at you and then you'd catch me looking. I was the one who wasn't ever able to speak," I said. 13-year-old me was actually feeling light headed. I'd spent most of junior high and at least the first year of high school working up the nerve to speak to Joe Stimpert. "And you never asked me out. I would have remembered. I would have gone."

"Yeah?" Joe was studying me, pushing Orville's hand away from his face each time the ape caressed him.

"And in the ninth grade you started dating Tina Myers. Then Abbey Millford. Jessica Hailey."

"Enough. Enough," he said, letting Orville ruffle his hair. "So maybe I found my confidence."

"Yeah, you did," I said. "And you never asked me out."

"Well... I always intended to," he answered.

The night sounds of Kansas grew loud around us, the chirping crickets, a chorus of bullfrogs celebrating some puddle of water somewhere in a ditch, a rustle of prairie grass, the sound of a semi-truck passing on the highway more than a mile away. The lights from Doc's jeep were growing brighter again.

Joe and I both jumped when a figure came at us from out of the shadows. It was the bearded lady. Orville rolled forward and hooted, jumping from the bed of the truck and rushing to greet her.

"Nope," she said simply, taking Orville by the hand and walking past the truck like she had somewhere to go.

"Well, at least the monkey's gone," Joe kind of laughed, watching the two of them walk away into the darkness together.

Doc pulled his jeep to a stop next to the truck. The other searchers crowded around. "No sign of them. Not the bearded lady or the tiger," he shouted to the group.

"The lady is back," one of the men answered. "She just went that way with the ape."

"Well..." Doc seemed to ponder a moment. "So just the tiger is missing. That's something."

"Go on home," he encouraged us. "Get some food, some sleep. Come back and help tomorrow if you can."

We hung on for a few more hours, but by one in the morning I was so exhausted I couldn't keep my eyes open. "Let's go home," I begged Zach.

Zach handed me the keys and stretched out flat in the bed of the pickup, making it obvious he planned to sleep on the ride home. I started for the door, but felt Joe's hand on my shoulder. "I can drive if you're tired," he said. So I shuffled around to the passenger door and climbed in the cab of the little red truck beside him. We bumped along till we reached a dirt road, then Joe drove slowly until we reached the highway. I rolled down the windows to keep myself awake. We didn't say anything all the long ride back to town.

13-year-old me was so busy chattering in my head, I wouldn't have been able to hear him anyway. "Joe Stimpert had a crush on you! Joe Stimpert always liked you, you idiot. You had a chance with Joe Stimpert, and you blew it." Apparently I'd blown it again and again and again.

At the clinic, Joe got out and I slid across the seat to the driver's side.

"Night, Jeni," he said to me.

"Good night, Joe," I said.

Then he did something unexpected. He reached out and touched my hair with his fingers. He drew back suddenly, as if just realizing what he had done and been caught a bit embarrassed by it.

"It's been good to see you, Joe," I said boldly.

"Good to see you too," he said, and I was grateful that he had to walk the length of my headlights to get to his car, cause it was one last chance to see all of him, top to bottom.

Chapter 6

There was a knock at the door the next day while I was taste-testing cookies for Zach's graduation party.

"That'll be Lisa," Mom said. "She's agreed to come over and help me hostess for the party so that I can relax and spend time with family," she offered in explanation. "She'll keep chip bowls full and serve people drinks. Just to help out, in general, so I can focus on visiting and Zach's big day."

"Sure," I said, but felt my stomach knot up. Too many years had passed. Not a day went by that I didn't feel some amount of sorrow at the loss of my childhood BFF. It was true, Lisa started it. There was no way around the fact that she had pretty much dumped me when she started dating Tommy. In recent years, however, I'd spent a lot of time dwelling on all the moments when she had tried to include me again. All the girls' nights she had planned our junior and senior year when I'd done everything in my power to lead her to believe I was too busy having fun with my new friends to dedicate any amount of time to her. Perhaps my anger at being jilted had been a tad bit overblown.

And it was I who'd thrown the barb that pretty much guaranteed the end of our friendship the day we graduated from high school. I was the one who had refused her request to take a picture of the two of us in our graduating gowns. I had turned my back on her so decisively and finally, knowing she was still within hearing range when I'd called her Tommy's whore and laughed with my new friends about what a loser she had become.

I still had the necklace that matched hers, half of a heart with the words Best Friends inscribed when you put them together. Sometimes, on my worst days, I would wear it under my t-shirt. It helped to remind me of the person I used to be.

Lisa followed Mom in the kitchen and sat beside me at the bar. Mom immediately made a plate with cookie samples on it and poured Lisa her own glass of milk.

"Just like old times," Lisa said, smiling as she glanced in my direction.

Mom watched the two of us, trying her third chocolate chip cookie, unless my count was off. "Well," she seemed to come to some decision in her head. "I have notes upstairs about the day tomorrow. I'll run get them. If you'll just wait here, Lisa. I'll be right back."

Lisa and I kind of swiveled on our seats in unison and watched Mom leave the room. I grabbed another cookie.

Lisa said, "So... you're back?"

I nodded, unable to lift my eyes from a series of miniscule crumbs that had somehow left my plate and fallen onto the counter.

"Listen," I forced myself to start speaking to get it over with. "Lisa. I don't know if it matters at this point... after so long, I mean."

More than anything, I didn't want to start bawling. I'd rehearsed this a dozen times in my head, and I thought that maybe I'd actually be able to get through it without losing control, but I felt the tears welling up in my eyes almost immediately. I blinked, caught my breath, and let it escape in a slow exhale. When I glanced up, Lisa was looking at me solidly, her head tilted a bit to the side as if perhaps her disgust with me had moved to pity. This made me feel all that much worse.

"I'm really sorry," I finally said. "It's inadequate, I know, but I really am. I'm so very truly sorry for what I said about you at graduation."

When I glanced up again I could see the pain in her eyes. There was a little part of me that wanted Lisa to be angry. I wanted her to chew me out, yell at me, inflict a little bit of pain in revenge.

"I was hurt," she said matter-of-factly. "But I know now that I hurt you too. I couldn't understand it for a long time, but I know I was horrible to you when Tommy and I started dating. I was stupid and young. There's no excuse for it. I never stopped to think how awful it must have been for you."

I looked up again and she was kind of staring off toward my mother's mixer.

"But I missed you, too. I started missing you a long time before we graduated. It just took me a while to figure out how to have

Tommy and to have girlfriends in my life. And by the time I got there, it was too late. You were already gone." She shook her head.

There was no use fighting the tears by now. Lisa's face was shining with them and I was pretty sure I was too. Just that quick, it was like we were standing on even ground again and I even believed we might find a way to be friends the way we used to be friends. I hadn't had a real girlfriend since Lisa. I'd had boyfriends. I'd known lots of girls in passing. But I'd never had another girlfriend who I loved and trusted the way and I had as a child, when Lisa was my BFF and I couldn't imagine my life without her.

"Sometimes I think…" I'd written these words a hundred times, trying to make sense of them myself. "Because I knew you so well and you were so much a part of my life, when Tommy came along and you were so into him, it was like a little part of myself was ripped away. A piece of me went away with you and I had to work so hard to be whole on my own without you."

Lisa just blinked at me. I couldn't decide if it made sense or not. "You always loved me and accepted me no matter what," she said. "I couldn't understand why you wouldn't be as thrilled about Tommy as I was. And then when I started to see what I had done, you pushed back and didn't want me in your life anymore. I thought you were just jealous for a long time. I thought you were being mean because I had something you wanted."

"To some extent, that's probably true," I whispered. "Not that I wanted Tommy, specifically, but a relationship like that. To have someone love me the way Tommy obviously cared for you. Sure. I was a little jealous. But more hurt that I'd become invisible to you."

Lisa turned back toward the bar and nibbled at a cookie. She dabbed at her eyes with her napkin and looked at me once more. "So we're both to blame," she said. "Would it be silly to ask if we could get past all that and be friends again?"

I wrapped my arms around Lisa and held her tight. "I don't think it's silly at all," I said. "I could really use a friend right now."

Chapter 7

The sun was full on shining in my room when I finally opened my eyes the next morning. It took me a moment to realize that it was my father standing in the doorway, clearing his throat gently just to see if he could rouse me without actually having to wake me up.

"I'm sorry," he said. That's when I realized he was holding the phone. "I didn't know if you would want to take this."

I sat up in bed. "James?" I asked, stifling a yawn.

Dad kind of shrugged and nodded all at the same time, holding the phone out to me with his hand still over the receiver, making it clear he was giving me a chance to bail if I wanted to.

I reached out and took the phone, pulling it to my ear. I listened for the breathing on the other end, conjuring James's imagine in my mind and trying to discern his mood and purpose before even saying his name.

"Hello?" I finally said, my voice coming out half force, not yet awake and ready for communicating.

"Good morning," the voice on the other end came through sounding much more chipper than I imagined it would.

"Yes?" I questioned.

"I just thought I'd see if you were going," the voice said.

"Well… yes," I said. I glanced up to see my father still standing there. He kind of backed up, apologetically, then turned and walked quickly from the room. "I am gone, James. I'm not coming back."

"Uh…" was all the voice on the other end could muster.

Somehow, this response emboldened me. Not only had James already missed me, he'd been silenced by the fact that I was gone.

"I know about her, James," I rushed on. "I know, and I shouldn't be surprised. I started out as the other woman, too. But I'm not going to be that person, James. I'm not going to be that woman who just follows you around the country and keeps your house and plays hostess for your parties and asks for nothing in return. I'm a person, James."

"Um," the voice on the other end was stuttering.

"I'm done. I know I should have said this to your face, James, but I wasn't even sure that you noticed I was still there. I took everything with me. I'm not coming back."

"Jeni. Stop," the voice said.

I rambled on—nonsense about perceived weakness and values and taking time to find myself—before it hit me. The voice had just called me Jeni. James had never, ever called me by my nickname. James had always called me Jennifer, and on occasion, when he'd had a bit too much wine to drink or was feeling particularly frisky, he'd call me his lovely, lovely Genevieve.

The sound of silence was deafening over the line.

"I'm sorry," the voice finally said. "It's Joe. I thought I'd see if you wanted to ride back out with me this morning. I was going to look for the tiger, and I remembered Doc Stueve asked your brother if he would work at the clinic today…"

I moved my mouth, unable to make any sounds come out.

"Jeni?" the voice said.

I swallowed hard, pulling the phone away from my ear. "Joe?" I managed to whisper. "I… I… I…" wanted to crawl into the back of my closet and die.

"I should have identified myself," Joe added, unhelpfully.

"I have plans with my dad today. Gotta go," the words came out in a rush before I could even think them. I clicked my thumb on the end call button and felt my breath come into my lungs all at once, making me shudder and gasp.

The shriek I felt inside my head must have escaped to my lips. Dad appeared back at my door looking worried.

"You said it was James," I said accusingly.

"I assumed…" My dad shrugged, looking sorry and confused.

"I… I'm such an idiot," I cried, knocking the phone to the floor and falling back into my pillow. I pulled my quilt over my head shouting again, "Idiot! Idiot! Idiot!"

"Jeni?" my father's voice was now close and rang with concern. "I'm sorry, Jeni. I just… I assumed it was James, calling."

"Caller ID? Did you not notice the caller ID showed a local number?"

My dad picked up the phone and looked at it curiously. "I never thought to look," he said, peering into the screen. "I just answer the phone when it rings. A man was asking for Jeni, and I didn't know of any other man that would be calling you."

I waited, but it didn't seem like Dad had plans to leave soon.

I slid the quilt down just far enough I could see him. His brow was crinkled with worry and his shoulders slumped with sadness. I felt terrible for making him feel terrible. "It's okay, Dad. Who else would it have been? You're right. I'm being stupid. I'm sorry, Dad."

Dad kind of smiled, but I could tell that he wasn't convinced and I really hadn't made him feel any better.

We stared at each other.

"So," he broke the silence. "Want to go try out the new coffee place with me on Wyatt Earp? Had you heard we're getting civilized? Cup O-Jones. It's a coffee house. Just like you had in Lawrence. Like Houston. Like on that television show, Friends."

I laughed. "I sincerely doubt Dodge City has a coffee house like on Friends," I said.

"Well, it's a coffee house. They serve all those drinks that you really don't recognize as coffee once you get them," Dad shrugged. "Get dressed. We'll go check it out."

Dad was busy making small talk as he pulled the bikes out of the garage and checked the air in the tires. I was having trouble concentrating on what he said, however. My head kept replaying my giant foible. I couldn't believe I had just handed Joe my whole sordid history with James in one stupid phone call.

"Jen? Earth to Jen?" my father had apparently been trying to get my attention.

"I'm sorry?" I asked, looking him in the face and forcing myself to tune in.

"I was just curious. Who was on the phone?" he shrugged like he was embarrassed to ask, and I knew I could avoid answering and wouldn't get any flack about it from him. My dad had always been content to remain in the dark about things, or to bide his time until mom filled him in later.

"Joe," I answered, watching for his reaction. Nothing seemed to register. "Joe Stimpert, Daddy. It was Joe Stimpert on the phone."

"Well, that's a name I haven't heard in a few years." A frown registered on his face. My dad had never liked boys like Joe. I suppose most daddies didn't think much of boys who plowed through girls like fish through water. And the Joe before girls, the Joe I'd had such a huge crush on in junior high, he'd never really amounted to anything that would have made my father's radar.

My father suddenly stood straight up. "Joe Stimpert," he said. "That's the boy who got the Shepherd girl pregnant your senior year."

I cringed, shaking my head. "Joe's done right by that kid," I said. At least, that's the way I'd heard it told.

"And he was with that Walters girl. What was her name? Addie?"

Addie Walters never stood a chance, as far as I was concerned. She'd grown up with parents I wouldn't wish on anyone. I didn't know anything about her history with Joe, but she had two kids before we even graduated from high school and it was rumored that at least one of them was by her own father."

"She got in trouble for manufacturing methamphetamine," my father said. "I think she's in prison now."

"I don't know, Dad, but Joe really doesn't strike me as someone who does meth," I said, thinking it probably wouldn't be a bad idea to make myself a list of questions for Joe.

I took my mom's bike from my dad and he placed her helmet on my head, pushing it down and adjusting the chin straps like I was a little girl. He put on his own helmet and dark sunglasses that covered his regular glasses. He swung his leg over his bike and coasted down our driveway in one fluid motion. I followed, taking a couple of blocks to get my legs warm enough to comfortably match his pace.

We rode side by side.

"You don't need to be involving yourself with guys like Joe Stimpert," my father said.

I opened my mouth, then closed it again, unsure how to respond.

"I've never been one to give you relationship advice," Dad was on a roll. "But maybe it's time I start. James was bad news. Anyone could have guessed that, but I held my tongue and let you make your own mistakes. But Joe Stimpert? Nah-uh. I'm sorry honey, but Joe Stimpert is not the kind of man you need to be involving yourself with."

My face was flaming. Anger. Embarrassment. Indignity. I wasn't really sure what I was feeling, but I was mad enough to consider knocking my dad from his bike. "You don't know Joe Stimpert, Dad," I said, unwilling to add that I really didn't know Joe Stimpert either "He just called because we were hunting tiger. It's not like we went out on a date or anything."

"I don't know? You don't know, Missy. Boys like Joe Stimpert are trouble. Boys like Joe Stimpert give the rest of us a bad name.

Just like James. Why are you attracted to men like that? What did I do wrong to send you into the arms of men like James and Joe?"

Dad stopped his bike suddenly, and I flew ahead before managing to get myself stopped. I was unable to turn the bike around gracefully, so after nearly falling head over heels when I caught the front tire on the curb, I swung my leg off and let the bike fall. I put my hands on my hips and approached my father.

"I... You... James wasn't..." but he was. I knew my father was right about James and it completely sucked the wind from me. "You don't know Joe Stimpert!" I finally blurted again.

My dad was shaking his head, looking somewhere between angry and sad. "Your mom and I did everything right. We gave you both trucks and dolls to play with. We encouraged your love of dresses and lace, as well as your love of climbing trees. You were unstoppable. You were the kid who was ready to take on the world. You lit up entire rooms with your energy. Hell, you made *me* feel like I could achieve anything."

"Daddy," I said. It came out in a hoarse whisper. My stomach was churning with emotions again. I couldn't decide if it would be more appropriate to scream at him or cry. What gave my father the right to take my failures so personally?

He put down his kickstand and got off his bike, reaching one hand out toward me. "I'm sorry, Jeni. That was... awful of me to say. I just... I just want you to heal and become yourself again."

This pricked at my heart and brought tears to my eyes.

I sat down on the curb, resting my forehead on my knees. My father sat down beside me.

"How long, Daddy?" I asked. "How long have you felt this way about me?"

"Oh honey. I love you. I..."

"How long have you thought of me as lost? How long have you been mourning the person I have become?"

Dad shook his head. I was expecting him to argue, but he just kept shaking his head. He pulled his cell phone out of his pocket and I thought for a moment that he might actually call my mom to ask for assistance, but he just glanced at the time and shoved it back in his pocket.

"I'm sorry, Jeni. I don't know why I said that. Joe Stimpert..."

"I don't want to talk about Joe Stimpert. I hardly know Joe Stimpert," I snapped.

After a long silence between us, I kept going. "I think you're right, Dad. I can't remember the last time I felt like myself. I used to have these dreams. Ideas. Plans. I don't know what happened to them. I worked so hard to do everything right. I paid attention in class. I put all my effort into every bit of homework. I got good grades. And the longer I did it, the less I understood my purpose in life. I lost myself, Dad."

I looked up at him. He was studying my face, listening to me with both ears fully engaged in the way that only my father has ever paid attention to anything I've ever had to say. He wrapped his arms around me and held me there on the curb. A Dodge City patrol car pulled to a stop in front of us.

"Everything okay?" the officer asked.

"We're fine, sir," my father answered. I raised my head and smiled at the man so that he'd know I wasn't in trouble. The policeman tipped an imaginary hat to us and drove off slowly. I felt him continuing to watch us from the rearview mirror.

"Joe Stimpert... we just met at the tiger hunt yesterday. It's no big deal, Dad. He was just calling to see if I needed a ride back out to look for the tiger," I said.

"And I'm not looking to start anything with anyone," I continued. "My last boyfriend doesn't even know I've dumped him," That part was bothering me more than I realized. Maybe I had expected that James would notice right away. Maybe I'd half hoped he would call me up, apologize, and ask me to reconsider.

"What do you say we head on down for coffee?" my dad finally asked after a long moment of silence passed between us.

I shook my head. "I'm really not in the mood," I said. "I think... I think I'd like to be alone for a while." I stood up and picked up my mother's bike. "I'm just going to ride for a while. Don't worry about me. I'm fine. I just need to clear my head."

I didn't even look back at him, I just rode away.

I rode south on Second Street until I reached the city limits and the city street turned to highway. It had been a while since I'd done any significant distance on a bicycle, but the land was flat and I found the peddling fairly easy. I rode and rode, doing my best to stay on the edge of the narrow shoulder of the highway without falling into the ditch. The passing semi-trucks felt enormous from this distance. As each one burst by me in a fit of wind and speed, I fought the wobble of my bike and kept my eyes straight ahead, determined not to let them scare me off the road. I thought about how easy it would be for one of them to simply veer a little to the right and squish me flat like so many bugs on their windshields.

I put my head down and pedaled as hard as I could, until the burn in my thighs was so strong and so deep that I felt like screaming. I wouldn't allow myself to coast. Pedal. Pedal. Pedal. Pedal. It became a meditative chant in my head.

I passed Quaker Road and Ridge Road. I kept my head down, refusing to look for the next intersection that would designate another mile. I passed the old school house at Saddle Road. My father had gone to school there as a boy. I'd grown up hearing stories of Richland Valley School House. It wasn't a one-room school, but a four room school housing grades one through twelve of country kids. They held classes there until the mid-60s, when they began bussing all the country kids to town.

It wasn't a terribly warm day for May, but the sweat ran down my face in rivulets, the salt started to sting my eyes.

"Turn around now," the voice inside my head said.

"Keep riding," another voice argued, more persuasively.

I pedaled and pedaled. The more the muscles in my legs protested, the harder I pushed myself. I covered mile after mile, until I began to consider that the tiger hunters were probably still out this direction. The thought of a potential run-in with Joe was more than I could handle. We'd been a few miles east of the highway last night when we had heard the tiger roar, so when I reached the next dirt road, I steered my bicycle to the right.

Riding on the dirt road was much harder than I anticipated. The road was topped with a deep layer of loose sand and the bike squirmed all over the place as I tried to pedal. My already severely fatigued legs were trembling with the effort. The sweat on my face had turned into tears. I got off the bike, took off my helmet, and started walking along the gravel road. It suddenly hit me that I was thirsty and the heat, which I had thought was mild at first, was beginning to feel borderline intolerable. I didn't have a cell phone on me, or even a watch. I estimated that I'd ridden for 10 or 12 miles.

In spite of all this, I kept walking the gravel road going west, away from the highway. Somewhere in my head there was a little voice screaming insults at me, but I ignored her. I wiped my nose on the sleeve of my t-shirt and stopped to use the bottom hem to wipe my face and brow. I let the pounding of my dusty tennis shoes on the dirt road mesmerize me. I listened for the thwap, thwap of the bicycle wheel as it turned beside me.

Tiger Hunting

I started counting my footsteps, anything to clear my head of thinking about the mess my life had become. 1, 2, 3… 101, 102, 103… 401, 402, 403… I wasn't entirely sure I'd kept accurate count, but when I hit 1,000 for the third time I stopped and looked at the horizon. Kansas didn't look all that flat from where I stood. I couldn't see the highway, but I could still hear the roar of the semi-trucks going down it at full speed. The sun was well into the western sky. My stomach growled, reminding me I had not eaten either. I turned in a circle, looking for a farmhouse, thinking it would probably be okay to knock on someone's door and ask to make a phone call.

I remembered Lisa pointing out to me when we were young that you could always tell where there were houses in the country because houses were the only places where any trees grew. I looked for clusters of trees. The three closest that I could see were so far off, I thought it might take hours to get there. I turned around and looked at my footprints on the road from which I had come. My best bet was to walk back to the highway. I could thumb a ride back to Dodge City. The chances that Joe Stimpert might pass on that particular highway at the exact time I would be walking it were slim, I assured myself. I was exhausted, thirsty, and tired. My mouth was so parched that I ached for water. I tried to work up some spit to no avail. I didn't even have a stick of gum on me. What had I been thinking? "You idiot," the voice inside my head said.

This time I watched my feet pound the dirt in order to keep one foot going in front of the other. The bicycle was cumbersome and the pedal kept smacking into the back of my leg. I cursed the bike, tried to push it further away from my body, but my arms were beginning to tire so badly by this time that the extra effort was too much.

I tried, briefly, to ride again. My legs would hardly go at all. I contemplated leaving the bike in the ditch. I could have Zach bring me back later to retrieve it. But then I considered that it might actually be easier to ride when I got back to the highway, and leaving my mom's expensive bicycle abandoned in a ditch might result in more dire consequences than either starving or thirsting to death.

Suddenly, goosebumps rose on my arms and I stopped. I felt her watching me before I even lifted my eyes from the dirt on the toes of my once white tennis shoes. She was standing right in front of me, maybe 15 feet away. She was panting, her tongue hanging out as if she shared my thirst. This was western Kansas, after all. It's not as if there were abundant ponds and streams dotting the landscape. I held my breath and stood absolutely still. My hands gripped the handlebars of the bike so tightly my knuckles started to ache. Her piercing blue eyes remained focused on me, as if assessing whether or not I provided an answers to her own hunger and thirst issues.

Chapter 8

I swallowed hard. The tigress and I stared at one another. She dropped to her haunches, licked her jowls, and continued watching me. I moved one foot, just slightly to the side, and she made a sort of mewling noise. Threat or greeting, I wasn't quite sure.

"Kitty?" I said softy.

The tigress flicked one ear. She was a huge and gorgeous animal. Had bars been between us, I would have been content to stand here staring at her for hours, snapping photos as I chatted with a friend, because nobody goes to the zoo alone. My mind wandered away from fear to contemplation. Had bars been between us, I would have had a snow cone. The thought made me salivate. A cherry snow cone, with a spot of clear ice where I had sucked all the sweet red juice away.

I drooled a little, and the tigress sprang up, taking three quick steps toward me before I yelled, "Kitty, sit!"

She stopped and obediently dropped to her haunches.

"See, she's a tame kitty," I said out loud. "No worries. Tame kitties don't eat people."

"Liar," the voice inside my head said. "Remember that circus guy? Roy Something-or-Other? Vegas entertainer? That was a tame kitty that took him out. A white tiger, too, if I remember correctly."

"Just stop thinking about snow cones," I scolded out loud again. The tigress looked at me expectantly. "Stop thinking about snow cones and everything will be all right."

The tiger sat, and finally I sat, as well. There was no chance I'd outrun her, I reasoned. I was exhausted and my body ached and my throat was so dry I wanted to cry, only I didn't have enough moisture left in all my body for crying. I couldn't muster the courage to try to move away from her, though it occurred to me she might walk alongside me like a dog. I talked to her, instead. I told her all about James and Joe and my parents and my life both before and after returning to Kansas.

It was getting cooler with the sun getting low in the sky and a steady Kansas breeze had picked up and was ruffling my salt-stiffened hair. I had been playing in the dirt as I talked, building little sand piles in a circle around my body. The tigress yawned and rolled to her side, taking her eyes off me for the first time since we'd met.

I watched her. She looked as sleepy as I felt.

I straightened my legs in front of me, wincing in pain and stiffness.

The tigress didn't seem to care that I was moving, so I slowly pulled my legs in and pushed myself to a crouch. When she still didn't respond, I stood up, my movements snail slow. The tigress stretched and rolled, batting her huge paws in the air like a playful kitten. She twisted in the sand, as if she felt a need to scratch a spot in the middle of her back. When she stopped moving, her eyes were on me again, but her body remained totally relaxed. Her eyes closed, opened, closed again.

"You're either going to die because this tiger eats you, or die of thirst and hunger," the voice inside my head said.

I bent over and picked up the bike. The helmet fell from the handlebars where I'd hooked it and the tiger startled a bit, but didn't leave her resting position. She started making a rumbling noise. I felt my skin grow clammy, and then it hit me. She was purring.

I always thought of purring was the sign of a content cat, but I thought I'd also remembered reading once that tigers did not purr. Whatever the noise, it didn't seem threatening. "Never trust a tiger," my little voice said.

I righted the bike and took one step. She blinked at me. I took another, moving toward the far side of the road. I stood for a long time watching her. She watched me for a while, then turned her eyes to the distant horizon. She looked past me, spied something in the ditch or field behind me. She put her big head back down in the sand and rolled back and forth as if inviting me to play.

One foot in front of the other, I began walking slowly, but steadily. At the spot where the tigress was laying, there was only about a foot of road for me to get around. Her long white tail slapped the ground. Tap. Tap.

I lifted my chin high and kept walking. Past the tiger, I allowed myself to pick up speed, but reminded myself that running might not be a good idea. If the tigress was playing a game of cat and mouse, I didn't want to encourage her to chase her prey. I just kept walking, ears straining to hear her pawsteps on the road behind me, ears straining to hear the passing trucks on the highway, trying to judge exactly how far away they were. I started counting my footsteps again. At 1,000, I finally allowed myself a quick glance behind.

The tigress was nowhere to be seen.

I felt especially vulnerable once back on the highway. The sun was down and only a sliver of moon was available to light the sky. It wasn't the big cat I worried about as much as my physical fatigue and the fact that half of the passing vehicles, if I was lucky some of the drivers would be paying extra careful attention, were likely zooming by without even seeing that I was there. I was prepared to hitch a ride. The idea of being kidnapped by a lunatic truck driver was far beyond any concern I could muster at this point.

I struggled with where exactly I should walk, close enough to the roadside that someone might run me over or deeper in the ditch where I'd be safer, but also less likely to attract a ride home. I was so dehydrated I couldn't even work up a sniffle to cry. I flung the bike into the weeds of the ditch. My legs were scratched from the brief stretch of tall grass I had waded through and the spokes of the bike were filled with thistles and dead, dry grass.

I flung my arms wide open and tipped my head up to the sliver of moon, letting out a strangled cry that would been more effective if my throat weren't so dry. I plucked a stem of grass with a tassel at the end, wondering if I might be able to suck some sort of nourishment from it. No such luck, and it tasted nasty, as well. Now I was suffering from dry mouth combined with taste of ditch weed.

I dropped my chin to my chest and let myself collapse into a heap in the ditch. I didn't care anymore. Let the tigress come eat me. Let a car run me over. Let me sleep here in this ditch with the chiggers and other nasty bugs. I closed my eyes and tried to void my thoughts.

That, of course, is when I heard the car slowing. I held still, trying to decide if my ears were deceiving me. There was a slight squeal of brake and the sound of a large vehicle being thrown into park.

"Hey!" a voice shouted. A vehicle door slammed and I heard some clunking and clanking.

Must be a pickup, I thought to myself. I opened one eye and peered toward the roadside where a full-sized white pickup truck was idling, two wheels full in the ditch, the other two right on the white line. My rescuer had arrived on a white steed.

A beam of light fell across my face. "Hey," the voice said again. There was rustling, the sound of boots wading through grass. "Are you okay?"

The voice didn't exactly sound panicked, but there was a bit of urgency to the questions. I opened both eyes and stared up into the night sky. The beam swept across me twice more before halting around my knees and traveling slowly up my body to my face. I pulled my arm across my eyes to keep from being blinded.

"I'm okay," I croaked. I tried to clear my throat and say it louder. "I'm okay!" This time it came out in a strangled kind of whisper-shout. I tried to sit up, but was having trouble commanding my limbs to follow the desires of my brain.

I finally managed to push myself into a sitting position when the toes of his boots arrived by my side.

"Jeni?" the voice asked. "Is that you? Oh my god." And then, "What the hell?"

I shook my head in my delusional state thinking maybe I could deny the reality that was happening. He squatted down and put an arm around my shoulders.

"Are. You. Okay?" he spoke slowly, perhaps thinking I'd suffered a brain aneurysm or been thrown from a moving vehicle. "Jeni? Jeni? Jeni?"

"I'm okay," I said again. The little voice in my head was scolding me. At the very least, I could come up with something a little more original. "My mom's bike," I said, pointing toward the weeds where I was pretty sure I had hurled the thing. "Can you put my mom's bike in the back of your truck and make sure she gets it?"

Joe released his hold around me slowly, backing and looking at me as if I was a truly odd circus animal, one more perplexing that an orangutan with a crush or a white tiger wandering the wilds of western Kansas.

"I saw her, Joe," I said, picking myself up off the ground.

"Your mom?" Joe asked, squinting at me. He moved toward the ditch and swished at the weeds with his leg. He located the bike and hefted it over his head in one swift motion. He carried it past me to the truck.

"No," I answered with all the sarcasm I could muster. "I saw her. I saw the white tiger. I met her on that road over there," I pointed to the intersection that was still closer than I had imagined when I turned back around to look at it. "I stood there for hours, face to face with her. She's out there. She's real."

"What the hell were you doing out here, Jeni?" Joe asked.

"I saw her," I repeated, thinking maybe he had not heard me.

"Were you out here looking for the tiger on your bicycle? Do you know how crazy that is?" Joe had his hands on his hips. A semi blew by and the wind whipped at us. Joe moved forward, took me by the elbow and half-guided, half-pushed me toward his tall truck. He opened the door and it was all I could do to pull myself up into the cab. I didn't allow myself to wince in pain until he'd closed the door again. I fumbled for the seatbelt and pulled it around me.

"Are you okay?" he asked, getting back into the driver's seat.

I stared straight ahead, thinking that of all the dumb luck, all the dozens of vehicles that might have passed on this road tonight to find me, Joe Stimpert was the one. It was my dad's voice inside my head this time. "Stay away from boys like Joe," he said.

"I'm okay," I answered, "But I really could use something to drink."

Joe had only a quarter of a warm can of generic soda in his truck. I drank it in one swig and then struggled to keep myself from gagging over it. We rode in silence and I watched the lights of the city of Dodge spread like a blanket over the horizon. I'd always loved this city at night. Every driving vacation my father had ever taken us on when I was a kid, I always looked forward to this moment, late at night, coming home exhausted from the bevy of activity that had filled our days in some far-off, exotic locale like Denver or Oklahoma City. The lights of the city twinkled with merriment and it would make me think of Christmas, a little city of lights under a dome of black sky. It was like a holiday, coming home, and I felt a rush of gratitude that after all these years, even arriving in the condition I was in, the town still looked beautiful to my tired eyes.

We hit the railroad tracks on Second Street and Joe moved his truck into the left lane, taking us toward the row of fast-food chains rather than right and then north again, the direction that would take me home. He pulled into the Sonic.

"Order?" he asked.

"I don't have any money on me," I stated bluntly, feeling imaginary tears well in my eyes and much-needed saliva pool in my mouth as I stared at the burgers and fries in the menu pictures.

"My treat," he said.

"An extra-long coney with cheese and onions, large fries, and a chocolate shake," I said without hesitation. "And a large soda – Sprite," I added.

"Okay," he nodded, a slight grin might have slipped onto his face. He reached through the window and pushed the red button.

"Bottled water? Don't they have bottled water here now?" I asked. "I think a bottle of water would be good for me right now."

"Welcome to Sonic," a chipper voice said over the intercom.

"One bottle of water," Joe said, then repeated the rest of my order verbatim, not missing a beat. He added a large cherry limeade and an order of fries for himself. He pulled a twenty from his wallet and laid it up on the dashboard.

We sat in silence, waiting.

When the carhop brought our food, I literally shoveled mine in. I had the shake half eaten and the coney dog entirely before I stopped long enough to thank him for the meal. "I can pay you back," I said after sucking almost the entire soda down without taking a breath.

I could tell that Joe was watching me from the corner of his eye, but I didn't really figure it mattered all that much. What could I possibly do in front of Joe Stimpert, at this point, that would make him think any less of me? I'd started the day by unintentionally spilling the sorry state of my love life and ended the day needing rescued, for reasons Joe still had no way to comprehend, from a ditch 15 miles south of the city.

Joe was probably thanking his lucky stars right this moment that his opportunity with me had passed when he was still too tongue tied to talk to a girl.

I stared out the window of his truck, not caring, shoving fry after fry after fry into my mouth.

"Round two?" he asked, pulling another twenty dollar bill out of his wallet. I was licking the salt from my fingers and sucking down the bottle of water. "I'll order anything you want. Never seen a girl get after a coney in quite that way."

He was grinning when I looked at him. I took a deep breath, trying to slow the ravenous quake that was still causing my muscles to quiver, feeling the food settle in, wanting to pull my eyelids down with it.

"I'm good," I said through a mouthful of fry.

Joe was daintily pulling his fries from the box, still half full, eating them in bite-sized pieces, seeming to savor every morsel.

"I'd like you to take me home now," I said. "Thanks for the food. The ride."

Joe studied a French fry. "Sure," he said, grabbing three from the box and shoving them in his mouth. He balanced the remainder of the box by his side, turned the keys in the ignition, and put the truck into reverse.

It was the Saturday night before high school graduation and Wyatt Earp Boulevard was a stream of cars going in both directions.

The blinker on Joe's truck made a tink-tonk, tink-tonk sound as he waited for a gap in the traffic that would allow him into the stream.

"So if I recall correctly," he said, "You got blasted drunk on the night before our high school graduation at the party at Stacey Metcalf's farm."

"I... You were there?" I was having trouble removing my eyes from his fries. I feared they might tip over when he finally hit the gas to surge into the line of traffic. He seemed to understand my preoccupation.

"I'm done with them," he said. "You're welcome to them."

I must have given him a blank look. I was so tired.

"The fries," he said. "They are all yours if you want them."

"Thanks," I managed to say, before swiping the box and stuffing the remaining fries in one fistful into my mouth.

Joe chuckled softly.

"So you were at Stacey's party?" I asked, feeling the least I could do was make small talk.

"Everybody was at Stacey's party," he said. "You really don't remember?"

"Well, sure. I remember the party," I said. "I just don't remember you being there."

"Wow," he said. "And here I thought..."

"You thought what?" I prompted.

"Well," he kind of shrugged his shoulders and tilted his face in my direction. "I thought we kind of shared something special that night. I'm just surprised that you forgot, that's all."

A rush of adrenaline kicked in. I felt myself sit upright, my eyes flying full open. "Special?" I kind of shrieked, and forced myself to repeat the word more calmly.

"Well you did kiss me," Joe said softly. His eyes were looking forward, watching the road with earnestness, his hands at 2 and 10 o'clock on the steering wheel. "And... that other thing, you know."

"I did not kiss you!" I shrieked again. "What other thing?"

"Man. That hurts," he shook his head. "I mean, it's okay. That you don't remember and all." He took one hand off the steering wheel and placed it over his heart. He turned the corner and kind of tilted his head toward the driver's door. A sob escaped.

"What?" I squeaked. "I did not... you... What other thing?" I demanded.

A louder sob.

I punched him in the shoulder.

"It's okay, Jeni. I'll get over it." Another sob burst from his side of the truck.

"You big faker!" I hollered. "You.."

Three loud sobs. He was still clutching at his heart and the truck wandered a little into the on-coming lane.

"Well, it was just a little kiss," he said, dramatically wiping a hand beneath his eye and sniffling. "But you put all that tongue into it and I really thought that it might have meant something."

"Bull. Hockey," I sputtered. "I never kissed you. You weren't even at that party."

Joe cracked. His face split into a wide smile and he started laughing. I punched him a couple more times on the shoulder, but the effort was almost more than I could muster.

"Want to know something true?" he asked as we bounced up the brick street that was Central Avenue.

I just looked at him.

"You hit like a girl," he said.

We rode a couple of blocks in silence before he asked, "You really saw that white tiger out there?"

"I did," I answered.

"And tell me again what you were doing all the way out there on your bicycle."

I shook my head. There was no use trying to explain it. I wasn't even willing to try. I leaned my head against the window and let my eyes close. It felt like only seconds later that the truck came to a halt. I opened my eyes to see that every light in my parents' house was blazing. There was a police car parked in the driveway and my mother was standing in the middle of the lawn. My father was already at the door of Joe's truck, pulling it open and pulling me into his arms in a breath-consuming squeeze.

"Jeni!" I think my dad might have been crying. "Where the hell have you been?"

I didn't even try to speak. I just let myself relax in my father's arms. He and my mother were on each side, pulling me toward the house, my feet barely touching the ground.

Jeni. Jeni. Jen-Jen. Jeni.

My brother, my father, my mother, and I think Lisa and her father from across the road were all there, a cacophony of voices, asking about my well-being, shouting questions about where I'd been. I found myself sitting on one of the white metal lawn chairs that had been passed down from my grandparents' house to ours. I could hardly track the faces that were swirling around me. Even the kindly old policeman seemed familiar, but I couldn't come up with his name.

Suddenly, a voice was close beside my head, whispering a message for me alone.

"You're right," Joe said. "You never kissed me. But I was at that party. Here's my proof. You were wearing black converse sneakers and those blue jeans you shredded yourself with a pellet gun. You had on a dark blue tank top and your red bra straps were showing. You called it your last show of school spirit, red and blue for the school colors. You asked if you could have a drink of my beer and you downed the whole thing in one chug. Then you told me that you'd been forever in love with me, ever since junior high home economics class. And I said, 'Wow. I didn't know,' and I gave you my phone number, but you never called."

Moments later I watched him walk across the yard to his truck. I glanced over to see my father pushing my mother's bicycle up the driveway. He was looking back towards Joe's truck, his brow furrowed. I closed my eyes and leaned back in the chair.

"I'm okay," I said. "I'd really just like to go in and take a shower and go to bed."

Chapter 9

It was my brother's voice that finally pulled me from the deep, deep sleep I finally dropped into sometime after midnight.

As soon as I managed to open my eyes, Zach said, "Sorry." He was sitting on the edge of my bed, looking every bit the kid brother I have always loved. "Normally, I'd be happy to let you sleep, but… you are planning to come to my graduation, right?"

"Of course," I said, trying to lift my hand to pat him on the arm, but I found the blankets sort of had me trapped. Every muscle on the right side of my body seemed to scream in agony with the effort of un-mummifying myself.

"Good," Zach grinned. "Grandma and Gramps will be here for lunch. Mom thought you'd want to come down for that, as well."

"Absolutely," I cried, working my left arm free of the blankets, as well.

"So, did you really ride Mom's bike out looking for that tiger?" My brother's face turned a slight shade of pink as if this question embarrassed him.

"No. Not exactly," I said. "I was just riding. I didn't really have a destination in mind."

"Man, Dad was worried sick. I don't think I've ever seen him so worked up about anything."

"I know. I'll talk to him."

"Mom kept telling him it was no big deal, that she was sure you'd stopped to visit a friend or something, but he was scared, Jen-Jen. I think he thought…" Zach stopped at this, his face deepening in color.

"Zach?"

My brother shook his head and looked away from me. "Nothing. No biggie," he said.

I watched my brother for a few minutes. He had fine fuzzy hair growing above his lip that was a little darker in color than I remembered it from Christmas when I'd last spent any significant time with him.

"How late is it?" I asked him, even the muscles in my neck felt sore. I could hardly lift my head from the pillow.

"11:30," my brother answered. "A little later, maybe."

"Grandma and Gramps are coming at noon?" I asked.

"Thereabouts," he nodded, and looked back at me. He stood up and stretched. "I'll leave so you can get dressed."

"Hey, Zach?" I said, stopping him. "Thanks for waking me. This is a big day. I wouldn't miss it for anything."

Zach nodded like he was heartily agreeing with me. "Jen-Jen?" he asked, taking a step back toward my bed.

I closed my eyes again and was working to get my eyelids to respond to my brain's request to re-open them. When I did, Zach was kneeling, his face just inches from my own.

"You would never..." Zach shrugged. "You know. You wouldn't ever..."

"What, Zach? Just say it."

"Well... hurt yourself. You wouldn't hurt yourself, right? I mean, you aren't depressed or anything like that, are you?"

I just stared at my little brother, my mouth open.

"Is that what Dad thought, Zach? Was Dad worried that I'd gone off and killed myself or something?"

Zach shrugged again, and the rosy color was back in his face, shining even across the top of his forehead.

I pulled myself forward, trying to sit up in bed. My stomach muscles protested. My thighs screamed. Zach looked a little puzzled. "Pull me up, Zach," I demanded. "Pull me up!"

Zach offered me his forearm, which I grabbed, then he pushed me from behind when it became obvious I didn't have the grasp to hold on.

"You okay, Jen?"

I laughed a little. "I'm just so damned sore, Zach. I rode a long way yesterday. No water. Got a little dehydrated and I rode a long, long way."

Zach laughed, too. I was finally sitting up in bed and had managed to untangle my legs from the blankets enough to get my feet to the floor. Zach sat beside me, a grin mixed with a little worry on his face.

"But hey," I said, seriously. "I'm a little bummed right now, and I honestly have no clue where my life is headed..."

I felt Zach suck air into his lungs. I thought he was holding his breath, truly worried that his sister was on some kind of ramp off the deep end.

"I would never do anything like that," I said. "I swear. I'm not in that place. I'm not even close to that kind of place."

"Yeah," Zach kind of whispered. "That's what I told Dad. I knew you wouldn't do anything crazy like that. He was just worried, that's all."

I held my little brother's hand, remembering when it was so small in mine and he had to, literally, look up to me rather than the other way around. I was looking forward to getting to know him, my grown up brother. He was a good kid, and it seemed like he was turning into a pretty good man. It made my heart ache a little to think of all the years that had passed when I'd simply been too busy, too involved in my teen activities to appreciate him or spend more time with him than I had. And then moving so far away after college. It had been a stupid thing to do, following James. I had never wanted to move so far from my family. I had never wanted to grow so distant from my own dreams. Now if I could only remember what they were.

The doorbell rang downstairs.

I released Zach's hand. "You better get down there. You know Grandma, she'll come with her billfold open for an occasion like this."

Zach smiled, "And then Gramps will open his wallet, never to be outdone by Grandma."

Gramps was my father's father. Grandma was my mother's mother. The two of them had been fairly competitive for our affection since I was fourteen. That was the year my other two grandparents had passed away. There was a little tiny piece of me that always wondered if my two living grandparents had developed a fondness for each other through the years. Grandma gave up her car a few years ago and Gramps always picked her up, from that point on, to bring her to family gatherings.

They teased each other endlessly. Grandma would scold Gramps anytime he stepped out of line, and Gramps would poke fun of Grandma's cooking on holidays, but in a very fun way, not truly criticizing or saying stuff that would actually hurt her feelings.

"See you downstairs," Zach sprang from the bed.

"Tell Mom I'll be a bit. I think I need a quick soak. Do you know if there's any Epsom salt in the upstairs bathroom?" I asked.

"I'll check," Zach answered. He sprinted from my room and jogged down the hall. I heard the clamber of cabinet doors and Zach hollered, "On the cabinet, Jen." Then I heard him start the water in the bathtub. "Better hurry," he said as he jogged back down the hallway, leaping down the steps in his every-other rushing fashion.

I stood, stretched as best I could, and managed to shuffle down the hall into the bathroom. The salts were sitting on the counter. I could see from the crystals in the bottom of the tub that Zach had already poured quite a bit in there. I filled my hand and dumped some more in. Then stripped and eased myself into the steaming hot tub. I couldn't decide if it was the temperature or the state of my leg muscles that hurt more. I just kept sliding in, slowly, slowly, until my entire body was submerged and the pain blended into something of a fog.

There was a soft knock on the door. "It's Mom," her voice called through the crack in the door.

"Come in," I managed to croak.

She was carrying a glass of water and two large pills in her hands. "Muscle relaxants," she said. "Your brother said it was something you might appreciate."

I put the pills in my mouth, and Mom helped hold the glass of water as I swallowed. I shifted so that I was sitting up straighter in the tub. "Fill that again?" I pleaded. Mom filled the glass in the bathroom sink. I drank it down twice before dismissing her.

"You good?" she asked, smiling in that gentle way she always did when she was taking care of me.

"Good enough," I answered. "Tell Grandma and Gramps that I'll be down soon. Just a few more minutes in here and I'll be down. Just a little sore, that's all. A few more minutes in this tub, those pills will kick in, and I'll be good."

Chapter 10

I startled awake when there was yet another knock on the bathroom door. I didn't know how long I'd been in the tub, but it was long enough the scalding hot water had cooled tremendously. From the goosebumps rising on my flesh, I guessed that the water temperature had just dropped below that of my body.

"Jeni?" It was my dad's voice this time. "Is everything okay? We saved a plate for you."

"Dad!" I pushed against the end of the tub and sat up straight. "I'm sorry. I fell asleep. I'm coming. Tell Zach and Grandma and Gramps that I'll be right there."

I was out of the tub and almost completely dry before I heard my dad walk away down the hallway. I felt terrible for making him worry so much. Other than feeling a little chilled, the state of my aches and pains had improved greatly. I wrapped in a towel and rushed to my room, throwing open my suitcase and digging for my dress clothes. I packed an outfit for easy access thinking that Zach's graduation would be one of the first major things on my agenda.

I'd forgotten to pull it out when I got here, however, so it was wrinkled and looked terrible. I dropped it on the bed and went to the corner of my room where a stack of boxes were balanced that mom and I had pulled from my car. Much, much more was piled in a jumble. My goal had been to fill my car to capacity, and not with convenient moving-sized boxes. The bottom of the stack, however, was the big box I had put in my trunk. This was the box I had used to empty out my closet in Texas. I'd dropped the clothes, still on their hangers, dumped in my few pairs of shoes and a half-dozen handbags on top.

By the time I'd dug down to find an appropriate outfit, my room looked something like a natural disaster. Hurricane came to mind, but then I scolded myself. I wasn't in Houston anymore. Tornados happen in Kansas.

Tiger Hunting

I still looked a bit wrinkled when I was done dressing, but far better than the suitcase-packed outfit had been. I slipped on sensible shoes—James had always been after me to wear high heels—and rushed down the stairs expecting to meet my family.

The house was quiet.

I felt my breath catch in my throat. How long had I been in that tub? I rushed through the kitchen and dining room and peeked in the living room, just in case they were being extra quiet.

Everyone was gone.

"Mom? Dad?" I called. I felt like a little girl, like the time I got lost at the mall, that sick feeling in the pit of my stomach when I realized, indeed, that I couldn't see anyone that I knew no matter what direction I turned.

I went back to the kitchen and looked at the clock on the microwave. I had about 15 minutes to get to my brother's graduation. They must have left without me. They must have decided I was sitting this one out. I was just about to dash up the stairs to find my keys, when the door to the house swung open.

"Jeni? You ready..." Dad shouted loudly, then kind of jumped when he realized I was standing right there. "Oh, there you are. I thought maybe you were still getting dressed. Ready to go?"

"You waited," I said, tears welling up in my eyes. I blinked rapidly, scolding myself for being silly and emotional.

"Of course I waited," he said. "Zach and Mom rode over with your grandparents. They'll save us a seat, but we'd better get going."

I grabbed my Dad's hand as I rushed out the door. I stepped close to him and kissed him on the cheek. "Thanks, Dad," I whispered. "I'm really looking forward to this."

Chapter 11

I'd probably been to half dozen graduations in the city's civic auditorium in my lifetime. Once upon a time, I would have sworn they were all absolutely identical ceremonies. Same girls dressed in red gowns and boys dressed in blue, walking across that big stage to be handed a diploma, a sign that you had succeeded in life thus far. It didn't seem to change until it was my turn to walk across. It struck me, I remembered, that for the first time, every kid walking that stage had a name. There were dozens of dreams being realized that day, and things were only going to get more interesting from there.

I think that was my first inkling that perhaps I'd gotten a bit lost. I remember sitting there, my mortar board on my head, smiling wide and thinking I'd made it. This little voice chipped in and asked, "Where? Where exactly have you arrived and where do you go from here?"

My breath grew shallow and I could feel my shoulders tensing up. I was headed to KU for college, that much had been decided, but what was I going to do there? Why had I selected KU over any other place? Had I even considered other options? I remained entirely clueless about what I might study and toward what goal I would be working once I was a high school graduate. I felt vastly unprepared and that feeling hadn't really gone away in the years since.

My friend Lisa had talked about going to KU all her life. Was that why I was going there? For so long I thought Lisa would go away with me and give up Tommy for a while, or at the very least, make him take a backseat while she went for a ride with me.

I began looking for Zach in the sea of mortar boards as soon as Dad and I entered the auditorium.

"Fourth row back on the right," Mom guided me with her words, "Eighth chair in."

There he was, his dark hair recently trimmed, yet sticking out from beneath his graduation cap. He must have felt me looking at him. He turned around and scanned the audience. His eyes stopped on mine and he grinned and gave me a great big wave. I stood up and waved back. I cupped my hands around my mouth and yelled, "Way to go, Zach!"

Gramps chuckled beside me and Grandma gave me a stern look from his other side. Mom and Dad were smiling and waving wildly, as well. When I sat back down, Gramps held out his jacket for me to see the inside pocket. He had one of those little hand-held air horns hidden. He winked at me, kind of tilting his head toward Grandma, making it clear that the air horn was our little secret. I could already picture Grandma knocking him upside the head with her purse when he blew it.

The superintendent of schools walked to center stage and the noise in the big auditorium immediately dropped to a low roar. The superintendent cleared his throat and the auditorium grew silent. It was almost eerie. Somebody sneezed from the seating high up. Someone in the group of graduates below giggled.

The superintendent began speaking and my mind began to wander, just like the old days. He kept his remarks brief, and then Mrs. Estling, the high school English teacher read one of those lists about what kids born in 1991 and 1992 have never known. This brought a few mild chuckles from the audience. I'm sure most had already seen this circulated via email. I was surprised at the number of "unknowns" that I knew. I was only six years older than Zach, but my first music collection was on CDs rather than an MP3 player.

I flipped through the graduation program. It still looked to be a product of the high school journalism class. I'd put ours together the year I graduated. It was a project I was really proud of; I read all the names at least a dozen times to make sure they were spelled correctly.

I was surprised to see the commencement speaker was Bethany Blaine. She was a senior when I was a freshman. She had a great voice and I knew she went straight to Nashville after high school graduation. I'd heard that she was doing well as a singer, but I didn't make it a habit to listen to country music, so I really wasn't sure just how big she had gotten.

She stepped out on stage, complete in country-western star attire. I cringed inside. I'd never gotten much mileage from the whole wild west theme that many Dodge Citians enjoyed. I hadn't worn cowboy boots since I was seven. Looking at Bethany now, I imagined she lived in them.

"Howdy! Class of 2009!" Bethany's voice was still lovely. "I am so honored to be here with you today. I graduated from Dodge City Senior High School ten years ago and I'm here to tell you, it's been quite a ride."

"Is she supposed to be talking about herself, or them?" Gramps leaned over and whispered in my ear.

Grandma gave us the evil eye, silencing me before I had a chance to respond.

Thankfully, Bethany kept her comments under ten minutes and then sang a lovely, upbeat country tune about what lies on the other side of the rainbow. Then we listened to a tiny girl in glasses, one of two class valedictorians, a first in DCHS history according to the principal, talk for about three minutes through a very rushed and high pitched speech. I wondered how she'd managed to get through speech class with a top grade. I would have failed her on nasal pitch alone.

Co-Valedictorian was Amanda Burney, my brother's girlfriend through most of his high school career. They'd ended it shortly before Christmas. Unlike the first girl, Amanda was gorgeous and curvy. She had wavy blond hair that fell around her shoulders perfectly. Her timing and her diction were perfect. I almost could have let myself be inspired by her speech, if the little voice inside my head had not kept going on about how naïve she was. I decided right then and there that I was glad Zach had dumped her.

"Glad we dodged that bullet," Gramps said after listening to Amanda's speech. I felt better knowing that Gramps agreed with me. Grandma elbowed him and furrowed her brow at me. I zipped my lips and tried to look innocent. It brought a smile to Grandma's face, but she turned away when Gramps caught it.

Finally, it was Zach's turn. As the Class Historian, a title bestowed after the entire senior class had the opportunity to nominate candidates and vote on it, Zach got the last word before everyone was handed their diplomas. He'd told me that he didn't even have any competition. His name had been the only one submitted in the nominations and 93% of his classmates had shown up at the polls to vote for him. Only one—whom he strongly suspected was his ex-girlfriend, Amanda—had noted no.

The superintendent introduced Zach and we sat waiting in anticipation. Gramps had reached inside his jacket, his hand at ready on the air horn. Zach didn't appear. I sat up straighter, peering as far into the corner of the stage as I could from where I sat. I glanced quickly over at my parents who were in the same upright position.

The superintendent cleared his throat and squirmed a bit. He took a few steps toward the edge of the stage, appeared to be talking to someone, and finally came back to the microphone.

"Zach will be with us in a moment," he said. "He had to stop to... uh, tie his shoes."

Mom's hand went up to her forehead. "Oh no," I heard her mumble. My father put an arm around her and squeezed.

"What do you suppose he's going to pull?" Gramps asked. "String bikini? Boxer shorts under his gown? Maybe he'll come out riding a tricycle."

The curtain at the side stage began to move. It looked like someone was shadow boxing it from the other side. There were a few giggles from the students on the main floor. My mother already had bright red cheeks. She was expecting the worst, I could tell.

Finally, one of the teachers jumped up and jogged to the side stage and pulled back the curtain for my brother. He came stomping out, in wild swimming trunks the color of ocean. He had giant flippers on his feet, a blow up child's floatation device shaped like a duck fit tightly around his waist, and he had on goggles with a snorkel sprouting from his mouth. His blue graduation gown billowed out behind him like a cape.

The graduating class roared with laughter. The audience of parents and family in the elevated seating area chuckled appreciatively. Gramps stood up and pulled the air horn from his pocket, sounding three quick blasts. It was so loud, I worried I would not actually be able to hear my brother speak.

Gramps set down, grinning, and Grandma jerked the horn away from him in seconds flat. She shoved it in her purse, causing another blast to sound. She smacked Grandpa on the leg for that one, as well.

Zach threw his arms up in a sign of victory. He brought them down and performed a little muscle man pose for us. He then did a pirouette, as well as anyone could who was wearing scuba fins.

Grandpa grinned from ear to ear and clapped. "That's our boy," he said over and over again. "That's our boy."

Zach finally made it to the podium. He took the snorkel from his mouth and pushed the goggles up on his head.

"So did you all hear? The circus came through town," he started. "They didn't come to town, of course. I still ain't figured that one out yet. It's been ages since we had a good circus show here in Dodge City."

The graduates cheered and clapped.

Tracy Million Simmons

"But that's okay," Zach said. "Turns out, those circus folk decided to stick around for a bit, and I had a little talk with them last evening, and one of them has agreed to help me out, and give us a little show right here at our graduation ceremony."

My parents both took this opportunity to look at me. I shrugged my shoulders in response.

"Everybody," my brother stepped out of his flippers so that he was now standing on the stage in his bare feet. "I'd like you to meet my new friend, Orville."

I gasped.

The orangutan walked out on stage. He was extremely upright, walking with every manner of dignity that my brother had managed to avoid. The ape turned for a moment and looked at the audience. He gave a very serious salute and then started grinning in his crazy monkey way and blowing kisses.

Gramps stood up and blew kisses back.

Orville walked the rest of the way to the middle of the stage and threw his arms around my brother. He puckered his lips for a kiss and Zach pulled back, thrown off his routine for a moment.

"Hey there, Orville," Zach said beside the microphone. "Orville. Orville? Orville."

It took Zach a minute to get his bearings. "Orville," he finally said. "I'd like you to meet everybody."

Orville turned and waved to the audience, flashing a mandatory grin and then turned his attention back to Zach.

"I'd say that ape has a thing for your brother," Gramps said.

"So Orville," Zach said. "These are my classmates, and they've elected me class historian, which means I'm supposed to come up with something witty and wise to commemorate our graduation."

The orangutan put one finger up to his lip like he was thinking.

"I thought about telling the story of Robbie Baker when he came to school with his sister's red panties stuck to the back of his sweater by static cling, but I wasn't sure that would be appropriate."

The graduates roared with laughter and most of the rest of the auditorium was filled with chuckles, as well. Orville shook his head like telling that story would be a really bad idea.

"No?" Zach said. "Well how about the time we played coed table tennis in phys ed and Marilee Dunn rushed into the boys locker room at the end of class and claimed she had forgotten she was on the boys side of the gym?"

More laughter from the students, and Orville shook his head decidedly against. Someone in the back of the auditorium yelled, "Go Marilee!"

"When Stewart Miller mooned the Garden City Football team?"

The ape placed one hand over his eyes.

"When Amanda Burney tossed her pom-pom at the opposing team's mascot?"

My brother and Orville went on and on like this through at least a couple dozen of his high school classmates. Most of the students kept laughing, but I could sense the rest of the crowd starting to grow restless. They were all inside jokes and, for those of us on the outside, these stories were too incomplete to be appreciated. My brother could get away with this because he was friendly to everyone and kind. My guess was that he spent a lot of time making sure he had a name to represent every demographic in the school so that the whole class would feel included. I loved this about him. And I loved the way he stood up in front of the crowd, so comfortable as if he was having a conversation with just a few of his closest friends.

His stories stopped abruptly and he turned uncharacteristically serious. "No really, it's hard to come up with something meaningful that connects all 347 of us graduating today."

Orville, sensing that his part of the routine was over, squatted, then leaned contentedly against the podium and stared placidly at the audience.

"We all have a lot of crazy stories from the past thirteen years. Most of us grew up here and we've been together, in a sense, from the beginning. Together, and yet I can guarantee that if we take a look at the people sitting next to us today, in front of us or behind us, there is someone you don't know well. Heck, maybe someone you don't know at all. Look at the faces around you. Is there someone you don't know? Be honest. We've been together, and at the same time most of us don't really know each other at all."

The chairs full of students below creaked and groaned as kids turned and looked at one another. The entire auditorium grew eerily quiet. I thought about my own high school classmates, the handful I'd been close to, and perhaps a couple of dozen I would have said I knew well and called friends. How easy it had been to walk away from all of them. With the exception of Lisa, perhaps, who I'd begun to miss even before I graduated.

"This is the end of our sheltered years together," Zach said. "From here, anything can happen. Some of us will get married and start raising families. Some of us will go on to college. Some of us will get jobs. Some of us—overachievers—will do all three of those things at once. Some of us will travel and some of us will stay close to home. Some of us will get the heck out of Dodge and never look back. Some of us will stay in touch. Some of us might just move on. Disappear. Shed this place for good."

There was a long pause and I listened as my grandmother took in a deep breath of air. I wondered if what was going on inside her head was anything like what was going on in mine. Remembering. Reminiscing. Missing, and being glad that it was all over at the same time.

"I guess what I'm saying," Zach took a step back from the podium and gestured at his ridiculous costume. "Is that whatever you do. However you do it. Don't forget to have some fun along the way. We may be grown up..." He pulled quotations from the air with his fingers as he said this, "but we shouldn't take ourselves too seriously."

At this point he looked out into the audience, searching with his eyes until he found me. Gramps patted my hand. Grandma picked up my other hand and held it in her own. Message received, I thought, suddenly over being impressed with my brother and feeling quite annoyed with him.

"Keep it real. Stay true to yourself. Have fun out there," he finally said, taking a deep bow. Oliver scrambled to his feet and bowed, as well. The monkey and Zach left the stage, hand-in-hand.

Chapter 12

Several guests had already arrived at the house by the time we got there. Lisa was at the door greeting people.

"I asked her to come over early and let people in," Mom answered, seeing the look on my face. "Not everyone was going to attend the graduation ceremony, and of those who did, I figured many of them would get out of there before us."

I came from a fairly large, very supportive extended family. It should have been no surprise that Zach's graduation day was going a major family shindig, but I was a little taken aback. I felt shy, all of a sudden. My Great Aunt Esther marched across our lawn carrying a huge package topped with a bow. About a half dozen second and third cousins played tag, shrieked and wrestled in the front yard.

I wondered how far back in the garage Dad hid Mom's bike thinking perhaps this would be an ideal time for another road trip. He seemed to sense my thoughts. Dad came around to the car door and opened it for me, reaching to take my hand. He pulled me to him in a tight hug.

"You good?" he asked and I remembered with guilt what Zach told me this morning. I smiled and hoped it looked genuine.

"I am, Dad. I'm just fine," I said.

My triplet cousins—Charise, Denise and Lanise—sat on our porch swing. They lifted their heads in unison and waved at us. "Hey, Uncle Darren, Jeni," they called. Though they'd changed their hair styles and colors tremendously, they still looked like carbon copies of each other. Same woman with different hair, I thought. They were two years ahead of me in school and I had spent much of my childhood longing to be one of them. No worries about where you fit in when you were enough to be your own gang.

I hugged each of them in turn, matching names to hair color. Charise was dark red, Denise was almost golden, and Lanise was a deep shade of black violet that seemed to change depending on the direction the light was falling on it.

The questions began almost at once. "Jeni, how is Texas?" "Where is James?" "What are you doing these days?" "Now did you decide on graduate school?" "Are you two planning your wedding yet?"

I seemed to be answering everything with a nod and a stupid smile. "Fine, fine, fine," I kept saying, though it wasn't always a fitting answer for the question. The triplets' father appeared—my Uncle Bill and his wife Veronica. My grandmother's sisters were soon clustered around me, as well as several cousins. I was so relieved when my brother showed up in his little red pickup truck. He had a girl with him I had never seen before. Both of my parents stopped, mid-sentence when they saw her get out. It was the girl from the circus I had seen that night with the dolphin. She was wearing a long flowing skirt, a swirl of colors that seemed to mesmerize the crowd in front of our house. Voices ceased, one by one, as all eyes were drawn to the pretty girl with enormous gold hoop earrings and shiny black hair that hung nearly to her knees.

I broke from the crowd to be the first to welcome them. "Congratulations," I whispered in my brother's ear when I threw my arms around him." Then I quickly backed off so he could introduce me to his friend.

Her name was Rita. She grabbed my hand like I was some kind of life raft as she watched the crowd from the porch descend on us. I took the opportunity to leave the crowd in the capable hands of my brother and pulled Rita into the safety of the house.

Immediately inside, we bumped into Lisa who was arranging gifts on the table. "Hey, Jeni," she said almost cautiously, eyeing the circus girl in a way that suggested she was trying hard not to openly stare.

Rita seemed to be catching her breath. "Big family," she said. "Zach said there would be a few people here. I thought maybe a half dozen."

I smiled. "Zach takes all this for granted," I said. "Aunts, uncles, cousins... everywhere you turn here there is someone you know."

"I can't imagine," Rita said.

"Kind of like a circus, only we don't travel together or entertain the masses. Only each other."

"Your family is like a circus?" Rita asked.

"Sure. Circus families. You're one big family right?" I paused, thinking maybe I'd blundered into offence.

"Hmm... right," she said.

I tried to pinpoint Rita's accent. Something about it suggested Eastern Europe, but I kept detecting a hint of deep south, as well.

"Is your whole family in the circus?" I asked.

"Lord no," she said. "Just me."

After a moment she added, "I don't have any real family, actually. It was just my dad and I once. But now just me."

"So the circus?" I asked, deciding her accent was definitely deep south.

"The circus," she shrugged, as if there was no more to be said about the matter.

"So," I was curious as hell about how she'd been invited to my brother's graduation party. "You and my brother?"

"Oh, Zach is a very nice boy. Very mature for a boy his age," Rita smiled and ducked her head.

I furrowed my brow, picturing my brother in the flippers and the duckie float toy just an hour earlier. "Yeah," I tried to sound agreeable. "I suppose."

Rita grinned and sat down on our couch. She leaned back, one arm throw across the back of it, the other resting loosely in her lap.

"Zelda. Bearded lady?" she looked at me for confirmation that I knew who she was talking about. "Zelda asked me to attend to Orville while your brother took him to graduation ceremony."

I felt a little bad that I had not thought to ask the bearded lady's name prior to now. "Ah," I said, as if that explained everything.

Rita pushed her ballet-slipper like shoes off her feet and pulled her knees up under her long flowing skirt.

"So tell me more about the circus," I said, sitting across from her in my Dad's favorite comfy chair. "How does one join the circus?"

Rita watched me intently for a moment. She bit her lip, and then seemed to relax as she began speaking.

"Well," she said. "I'm supposed to tell you about how my family has been in the business for generations. Gypsy folk. Romanies. What have you." She lifted the hair that was cascading over her shoulder. "I'm just a brunette. This black is hair dye. I have to color it at least once a month to hide my roots."

I raised my eyebrows.

"Don't get me wrong. Most circus folk, they have been in it for generations. Maybe not the big circuses like Ringling Brothers, but sideshows like ours. There're all carny-folk. Grandfathers and fathers, brothers and sisters. The little boy in our act…"

"I haven't actually seen your act," I interrupted.

"Oh yeah… well… the rest of them have gone on. Gimano, he's the ring master. His son trains the animals and his other son works the trapeze with me."

"Gimano who was driving the trailer that ran off the road?" I asked.

Rita's eyes widened and she bit her lip again. "I probably shouldn't talk about it," she said.

I quickly changed the subject. "So you don't come from many generations of circus folk, where do you come from?" I asked.

She only hesitated a few seconds before continuing. "Mansfield, Texas," she said. "I was a gymnast in high school. A pretty good one."

"And what? The circus came to town and you ran away with it?"

Rita shrugged. "Yeah. Pretty much."

"Seriously? I thought that only happened in novels and in movies."

Rita shrugged again. "The inspiration for every piece of fiction has to come from somewhere."

"So, how long have you been in the circus?" I asked.

"Since I graduated from high school. I just really felt the need to get away. It wasn't really planned, but, yeah, I kind of hid in one of the trailers as they were passing through town. Orville manipulates the locks on his cages at will. He let me in. It's kind of funny, because he's usually a huge tattle tale when people are around who aren't supposed to be. But when I showed up, he just reached his hand through and pulled out the lynchpin. He made a little bed for me in the corner. I got fleas. God that ride was awful, but he seemed to understand that I needed a way to escape."

I studied her, trying to imagine myself crawling inside a circus wagon, riding off into the night and reinventing myself as a circus princess.

"Sounds kind of fun," I sighed. "I used to be pretty good on a trampoline. Would the circus have a spot for me?"

The house suddenly filled with chatter and I turned to see most of my relatives following Zach into the living room. Mom and Lisa carried trays out of the kitchen and organized them on a long table at the end of the room.

"Maybe we should go help out in the kitchen," I said. Rita nearly jumped from her seat and followed me, the energy of the crowd pushing us toward the quiet solitude of the kitchen. I grabbed a spoon and started stirring the cheese sauce in the crock pot.

"How can we help, Mom?" I asked when she came bustling back into the kitchen. Mom grabbed a spatula from the drawer and hustled out again.

"We're good, honey. You enjoy yourself. Everyone is looking forward to seeing you, too."

I looked around the kitchen in a panic, finally settling on the kitchen sink where a number of dishes used in preparations were beginning to pile up. I filled the sink with hot water and soap and began to meticulously wash each measuring spoon and bowl. Rita came to stand beside me and she rinsed. I thoroughly de-cheesed the cheese slicer. I scrubbed a pizza pan until it was nearly as shiny as new. Rita dipped her hands in and out of the water, patiently waiting until I gave her each new item to rinse off.

"Do you like it?" I finally asked, sensing that she didn't really want to share why exactly she'd felt compelled to run off and join the circus in the first place. "Flying through the air with the greatest of ease? The daring young girl on the flying trapeze?"

She half-shrugged. "Yeah, I do," she said softly. "It might sound kind of silly, but there's so much freedom in the circus. We practice a lot, but there's also lots of time to read and study. I've learned more in my time in the circus than all my years of school together," Rita said. "No teachers jamming facts down my throat. No parents telling me I should be this or that. I'm just me. Rita. And there are no limits in my world. No boundaries."

"What about money?" I asked. "Do they pay you well?"

"It doesn't work that way in a circus family," she answered. "Everybody contributes what they can, and in return everyone is given what they need."

"Like communism?"

She made a little hem-haw motion with her head. "I suppose," she seemed to be thinking about it. "More like, just... I don't know... family. It's like the way a family should be. All watching out for each other, taking care of each other, doing what they can to make life easier for each other."

"So what do you do besides swing from the flying trapeze?"

"I help care for the animals. I tutor Peter, Gimano's grandson. I fix meals. I read to Grams, Gimano's mother, because she is old and going blind."

"Nice," I said, wondering again if there might be a place in the circus for me. I couldn't see myself on a trapeze, but I had just proven that I could ride a bike for long periods of time. Perhaps I could dress up as a clown and ride round and round the ring in circles.

Twice Mom came in, urging me to escape the kitchen and socialize.

"Soon," I chirped the first time.

"Your parents seem very nice," Rita said. "You have a nice family here."

"Yeah, they're not bad," I admitted.

Mom rushed in again.

"I'll be right out," I stalled again. My mother was a sucker for the language of agreement. I knew that by going along with her request, in at least a verbal manner, I could delay my kitchen departure much longer than if I told her the truth, that the whole idea of conversing with so many extended family members was making me anxious and that I didn't want to talk to anyone about me, my relationship with James, my lack of a career and my life in general at this particular point in time.

"Sometimes you have to clear the hurdle and move forward," I heard Mom's voice in my head. I swallowed and blinked back tears. Is this what I had really come to do? To hide in my parents' kitchen and dream about running off with the circus?

I could be useful here. I could be my parents' housekeeper. I could live in my old room and read novels all day long. I could take my Mom's bike on long rides through the country. Maybe take a camera along and capture the beauty of western Kansas.

I could join the circus, if they'd have me.

I could get lost. I could get eaten by a tiger.

The possibilities were endless.

Chapter 13

I felt a little bad after Zach's party. I used Rita the entire evening as a buffer between me and my extended family. When Uncle Charles asked about life in Texas, I said, "Rita is the trapeze artist with the circus, Uncle Charles. You used to parachute from airplanes in the army, right? I bet you know a little about flying high." And Rita would engage Uncle Charles, or whatever relative she was shielding me from, in small talk about this and that. We didn't exactly make a deal, but she seemed to intuitively understand that this is what I wanted from her.

Zach made a point of bumping into me a few hours into the evening. "You've stolen my date," he accused. "What's up?"

"Rita?" I feigned innocence. "Just checking her out. Making sure she's good for you."

"And?" Zach sat down heavily on the arm of the couch, staring across the room at Rita like a love-sick puppy.

I watched her, too.

"Well?" he finally said. "What's your conclusion? About Rita?"

"I really like her, Zach," I said honestly. "But she's a traveling girl. A circus girl. She's on the move, and I think there's something there. Something she's hiding."

"You don't think it's like… a boyfriend she's broken up with, but he doesn't know," he had his arms crossed, a finger resting on his lip and his brow furrowed deeply.

I smacked my brother hard on the arm.

"You know she's not Eastern European, right?" I asked.

Zach kind of shrugged. "I'm not sure I thought she was eastern European," he said. "We've just talked about, you know, otters, the dolphin, the giraffe and stuff like that."

"Orville," he added after a pause. "We've talked a lot about Orville. That ape is crazy!"

Rita took a breath from telling stories to my Aunt Velma who was admiring Rita's colorful skirt. Aunt Velma was one of those silver haired ladies who managed to add a cast of blue, a cast of purple, or a cast of pink to her ancient locks on a regular basis. From their body language, I would guess that Rita was a fan of today's teal.

I saw my mother's eyes fall on Rita a couple of times. It always seemed to knock her a bit out of her element. She'd look at the beautiful gypsy girl there in her own house and seem to lose her words or her direction for a moment.

"So hey," Zach said. "You know what a gap year is?"

"Sure," I answered. "It's something privileged kids do. Take a year between high school and college to backpack through Europe or something."

It was a subject James had ranted about frequently in recent years. He was so tired of trying to teach something to all these privileged kids who thought their one year of kicking through old churches and ruins rivaled his years of in depth study and contemplation. At least, where English literature was concerned, which was James's specialty.

"It's not just rich kids," Zach said. "Lots of kids who plan to go to college are making a deliberate choice to hold off a year, make some money maybe to pay for it, or just spend some time exploring and trying to figure out exactly what they want to accomplish once they get there."

I kind of shrugged, trying to wrap my mind around what Zach was saying.

"You're not thinking about joining the circus, are you?" I asked, looking at my brother, who seemed to only have eyes for Rita. If he said yes, I was going to kick him for stealing my idea.

Zach didn't answer.

"Zach. Seriously. Mom and Dad would have heart attacks. You've got your scholarships all lined up."

"Maybe not the circus," Zach took a breath and seemed to be drawn back to reality a bit. "Not the circus, per say."

I shook my head. "No way, Zach. You'll go to college just like I did. That's what they've been planning since the day we were born. Hell, since before we were born."

"That's just it, Jen," Zach took his eyes off Rita enough to look at me. His face was all earnest, almost pleading for me to see his side of things. "They've been telling us for years how things are going to be. Everybody is always telling us what we should do, how we should do it. And is college really any different? Isn't it just more of the same? Study this. Study that. Do this. Do that. This is the way we go to school, go to school," Zach started singing the children's nursery rhyme that I was thinking usually had something to do with washing clothes. He started low, but then started singing it loud to the whole room. Conversation ceased. All eyes were on Zach, and therefore me as I was standing right beside my brother.

The family was silent, but Rita took up the beat and began a little hip shake and shudder. She lifted her hands to clap and her bangles jingled.

"This is the way we go to school, so early in the morning," Zach sang. "This is the way we get our diploma, get our diploma, get our diploma."

Rita met Zach half way and they began a slow twirl together in the middle of the room. When Zach circled round so that he was approaching me again, he let go of Rita's hand and grabbed mine, forcing me to do his little circle dance, too.

My Aunt Velma and Uncle Charles sort of picked up the beat. Aunt Velma had a bum hip, but she had the shudder part down almost as well as Rita. Charles was a master of clapping, if not rhythm.

The energy in the room picked up, but my parents remained standing still and together, looking perplexed and confused.

Zach made up a couple more rounds of his song. "This is how we spell success, spell success…" Finally, he stopped singing and held up his hands. This brought applause, which launched Zach into a round of bowing and gratitude.

"Actually," he spoke, but the crowd took a moment to respond. He held up his hands again and shushed the crowd. "Thanks, everyone. Thanks a lot for coming today and celebrating with me. Damn! It's good to be done."

Polite applause erupted again.

Mom came to the center of the room and hugged my brother. Dad came too, patting him on the back. The two of them grabbed each other in a great big bear hug, and Zach ended up with one of my parents under each arm. My parents weren't short, but my brother was easily a good six inches taller than either of them.

"Mom. Dad." Zach was speaking so that the whole room could hear. "I want to thank you two most of all. You guys have been there for me, supporting me every step of the way, always expecting the best from me and, uh, gently encouraging me when I didn't expect the best from myself."

Mom and Dad were both beaming. I shook my head subtly, trying to catch Zach's eye.

"Mom. Dad. I have an announcement."

Something in Zach's tone made my mother look at Rita. Her eyes were wide as if looking for a fire she could smell, but couldn't quite pin-point the location. She looked at me. Zach. My dad. Gramps. And back to Rita again.

"Look," Zach said. "I've got some great scholarship offers and I know a lot of you have given me cash by the look of all those envelopes on the table." He winked at me, refusing to heed my warning.

"I want you to know, first of all, that I'm banking all of those gifts for college."

Cheers broke out in the room.

"You can buy gas for your car with mine," Uncle Charles yelled. Uncle Charles owned a line of gas stations and I presumed he'd given Zach a pre-paid gas card like he had given me, with a couple hundred dollars for gas on it.

Zach smiled and went on talking. "I guess what I want you all to know is that I appreciate everything each of you have done to support my education and I do plan to go to college… some day."

This is where my father got a look on his face like Zach had punched him in the gut. Zach squeezed my parents' shoulders a little tighter as if willing them to remain upright and remain solid beneath the news. Mom still had a smile on, but it somehow seemed frozen in place.

"I'm taking a year off," Zach continued, "Before I go to college. I'm not exactly sure what I'm going to do, yet… where I'm going to go or what I'm going to accomplish. But really, that's kind of the whole point of the exercise. For one year, I vow to follow nobody's compass but my own."

The room was completely silent. Many of my relatives found sudden interest in lint on their sleeves or spots on their shoes. Everybody in the room avoided making eye contact with my parents. Only Rita seemed to be unfazed by this news from my brother.

"It's going to be great," Zach made a feeble attempt at closure. "I'm sure there's a ton I can learn. It's a learning opportunity. It's a…"

"The world will be your classroom, Zachary," Rita's soft, melodic voice rang through the room.

Chapter 14

After the party guests cleared out, my parents spent the next several hours trying to convince my brother that he had been misguided. I invited Rita out on the porch and when the level of conversation breached the walls, we ended up across the street on Lisa's porch. Lisa brought us glasses of iced tea. Rita took a sip and wrinkled her nose.

"You forgot the sugar?" she asked.

Lisa laughed. "I can get sugar. We just don't dump it in automatically around here."

When Lisa came back out with a sugar bowl, Rita dumped a couple of generous teaspoons full in her tea and stirred. "So you are married, Lisa? You have children?" she asked.

Lisa kind of glanced sidelong at me before she answered. "Yeah, married with three kids. Always thought I'd be a college girl like Jeni here. But I went and fell in love."

Rita looked from me to Lisa and back again.

"So are you happy? Married with children and still in love?"

Lisa shrugged. "Sure," she said. "I mean, I guess."

After a moment she continued. "Don't get me wrong. I am so in love with my kids. I can't imagine my life without them. And Tommy... well, he's grown up a lot." Lisa looked at me as she said this part. "He's a good man. He's completely devoted to me and he adores his children. I'm really fortunate. I know a lot of people who get married young and it doesn't quite turn out this way. But it has worked for Tommy and me. We've worked hard to make it work."

I tried to picture myself for a minute, happily married with three kids. I still felt like such a kid myself. Was that what separated Lisa and me? Not the fact that she had Tommy, but the fact that she had matured out of my range?

I felt my cell phone buzz in my pants pocket, followed by the audible chime that meant a text message had been received.

Lisa and Rita both looked at me expectantly. I kept my eyes locked on the picture window of our house across the street where I could see the silhouette of my father pacing, my mother's hands occasionally clawing at the air.

I sighed and pulled the phone from my pocket.

tennyson? copy not on shelf. did u move it?

I deleted the message and shoved the phone back in my pocket. "It's my damned copy of Tennyson," I mumbled. "Of course I moved it. I've moved!"

Lisa and Rita both stared at me.

"Everything okay, Jeni?" Lisa placed a hand on mine and I squeezed back, the way we'd done a thousand times when we were kids. I squeezed my eyes shut, blinking back the tears that threatened to rush forward.

"That was James," I finally said.

"You're fiancé," Lisa said, matter of factly.

I laughed. "Not exactly. James and I are not engaged. James doesn't believe in marriage."

"Oh," Lisa sounded apologetic. "I guess I assumed. You moved to Texas with him, I thought you two would get married eventually."

"James isn't the kind of man I would marry, anyway," I said bitterly.

"Then why did you move to Texas with him?" Rita asked.

"I don't know," I answered truthfully. "It seemed like the thing to do at the time. I wasn't the only one doing it. The crowd we ran with, the crowd James ran with, they were too sophisticated for marriage. It wasn't the thing to do."

"Huh," Lisa said, as if this might or might not make some kind of sense to her. "I couldn't wait to get married."

She'd barely turned 18. She and Tommy had walked down the aisle in June, only a month after our high school graduation. I'd been one of the bridesmaids by default, even though I'd already felt that Lisa and I had become strangers.

"I would like to get married someday," Rita said. "But I'm not in any hurry. I want true love to sneak up on me, surprise me with its strength and power. But I want to be so rooted in myself that I don't sway to the breeze of just any man. My husband and I will choose to make our steps in time together because we respect and honor each other."

I wondered what a girl who ran away from home to join the circus could possibly know about roots. I longed for poetry like Rita's words to rise in me spontaneously and describe the way I felt.

"I started having an affair with James while he was seeing someone else," I blurted. "I never really intended for it to be that way, but by the time I realized... I mean, truly understood that I was the other woman, I guess it had gone far enough I couldn't stop myself."

Rita looked at me thoughtfully, but Lisa was staring at me as if her whole perception of me had changed.

"He was married?" she asked, unable to mask the horror in her voice.

"No. I told you. James isn't the marrying kind of man. But he had a girlfriend. Someone like me. Someone who lived with him and probably loved him." I'd never really thought about this last part before, but it had to be true. I thought about the way her shoes had been tucked beneath the bed that first night I spent with James. I could still picture the medicine cabinet the next morning, when I'd pulled open the mirror and the realization had slowly dawned on me. A woman lived there. I had crossed some sort of line that I'd felt must be sacred, but because I'd crossed it, I was somehow able to downplay its significance in my mind. I felt Lisa's revulsion. Sleeping with another woman's boyfriend was a slutty thing to do, a thing that girls who had no morals, no guiding principles would do.

"Wow," Lisa was staring straight ahead, as if unable to look me in the eye. "I never imagined. I mean – not getting married. I can picture that. I understand you waiting. But an affair. Wow."

It sounded incredibly self-righteous, but in my heart I knew I agreed with Lisa. I, too, came from a world where you loved the man you slept with, where it was wrong to take what belonged to others, and when you made a mistake, you paid your reparations, at least in guilt if nothing else.

"James is seeing someone else now," I said.

Lisa's eyes went wide. "What are you going to do?" she asked.

"I've already done it. I've left him. He just," I stopped, asking myself why I was confiding all this to Lisa and Rita.

"Good for you," said Rita.

I allowed myself to laugh a little. With a snort, I said, "He doesn't know."

"Doesn't know what?" Lisa asked.

"He doesn't know... he doesn't understand that I've left him. He's been text-messaging me since I left Texas. Asking if I'll be home in time for such and such party, or if I can tell him where the artichoke dip recipe is. Just now, he's telling me that the Tennyson book is missing from our bookshelf. It's missing because it's mine. All of my stuff is missing and the Tennyson book is the first thing, after four days, that he has noticed is gone."

"What an ass," Rita exclaimed.

"No kidding," Lisa gasped, "Jeni, what were you doing with this guy?"

"That's just it," I said, the tears bubbling back up in my eyes. "I've been on some kind of autopilot mode since college... hell, maybe since high school. I don't know why I was with James or why I've done anything that I've done in the past six years, for that matter."

Lisa grabbed my hand and squeezed again. "It's okay, Jeni," she said. "I've been there. Maybe not for six years, but I know what it's like to lose your compass."

"We've all been there," Rita agreed.

It was well after midnight when my father stepped out on the porch and sat himself down in the swing. Lisa and I had given Rita a ride back to the clinic where she was apparently staying, along with Orville and the bearded lady and half the circus menagerie. I'd offered her our guest room, but she'd thought my parents and Zach might need a bit longer to recover from Zach's momentous news of this evening.

Lisa and I talked quite a bit about her kids, her life with Tommy, the difficulties of taking care of her parents now that her mother's health was going downhill. She'd tried to pry information from me about my life, as well, but I was already feeling so tender and exposed. I didn't want to think about myself. I just wanted to hear about a normal life.

We were silent, both watching my dad on the swing.

"You think Zach is right?" she asked.

I shrugged. "My brother pretty much always gets his way. Who's to say if he's wrong or right? He's just stubborn-headed enough it doesn't much matter."

"It's not alright with your folks, that's for sure," Lisa looked at me.

Tiger Hunting

"I think they are afraid that if he doesn't go to college now, he never will. It's always been important to them that Zach and I have the opportunities they didn't."

Lisa nodded her head in agreement. "I always thought I'd go. And look at me now."

"It's not like your window has closed, Lisa," I said.

"I don't even know where I would fit school right now," Lisa said. "I mean, I know people do it all the time, married with kids and all, but I'm so busy as it is I don't hardly have a moment to myself. How would I fit in going to class and studying for the test and doing homework?"

"Maybe later, down the road. Maybe when your kids are older," I said.

"Maybe," she shrugged.

"I should have taken a gap year," I mumbled, thinking about the words my brother had used to present it. "It's about time I learn to follow nobody's compass but my own."

It was eerie, how much Zach's words sounded like Mom's. Yet they were on opposite sides. In Mom's world, we'd go to school and come out with our compass pointing us in the right direction. She really believed that college was an answer, a way to get where you needed to be. I had failed in that respect.

"So you and Tommy have done okay? You happy? You like being a mom?" I wanted to change the subject quickly. I wanted to stop thinking about where I'd gone wrong.

"Oh, Jeni. I love being a mom. It's bigger and better than I ever imagined it. Not always easy, but I can't imagine my life without them."

"But you have imagined? Maybe just a little bit?"

She smiled. "Oh sure, like when everyone has got the pukes and I've not been able to sleep solid for days and Tommy's stressed because they've got him working overtime. I've had my moments, dreaming of being carefree like you."

"Oh yes, because I live such the dream life."

"Well... we have fallen out of touch. But I think of you often. I keep up with what you are doing through your folks. Your dad and I talk nearly every morning when we step outside to get the paper."

"Just like our dads used to when we were kids," I said.

"Yeah. I get the paper for Daddy now. He's so busy worrying over Momma. He forgets to take some time for himself, so I go get the paper each morning and make him coffee and make sure that he sits for a few minutes before getting Momma up."

"How about you? Who is watching you to make sure you get time for yourself?"

"Oh, Tommy's real good about taking the kids in the evenings and he helps Daddy with Momma on weekends. And besides, I'm young. I have energy that Daddy just doesn't have these days. My folks are older than yours, remember? And then with Momma's health being what it is. It's just crazy and busy, but I cope. I do all right."

I realize that she's got tears pooling up in her eyes. I hesitate only a moment before putting my arm around her shoulder. We lean our heads together and just sit there watching my father on the porch swing across the street.

"So are you really going to stay for a while?" Lisa finally asks. "Cause it sure would be good having you around again."

"I think I will," I whisper. "I don't know where else I'd go."

Chapter 15

Daddy watched me cross the street. He looked tired and slid over on the porch swing to make room for me. "You probably want to be calling it a night," he said softly.

"Nah. It's still early," I answered. I sat down and snuggled up to him the way I'd done a million times before. "You okay, Dad?"

My father sighed deeply. "The thing is," he finally said. "What Zach says makes a lot of sense."

"Zach's a smart kid. He'll do okay," I laughed, giving my father's arm a squeeze.

"But try turning your mother's mind around," Dad said. "She's had it planned for you two since before you were born. Your lives mapped out. We were saving for our kids' college educations before we even knew how many kids we were going to have."

I thought of my mother's map and her speech about my compass and the way she'd always been so good to listen and not interfere in my decision making, yet I had always known intuitively, exactly what she expected from me.

"Why didn't you and Mom go to college, Dad?" I asked. I thought I knew the answer, but wanted to hear it with my new and growing perspective.

"I don't know that we really had an option," Dad said after some thought. "Money was tight for both of our families and running out and getting a loan like kids do these days was out of the question. My family didn't believe in borrowing money, and your Mom's family… Well, she couldn't have gotten a loan for herself, and her father simply never would have signed off on one."

"Why not?" I asked.

"Oh lordy, Jen. So much has changed in this world. Your grandpa, he was an old fashioned kind of guy. He wouldn't have spent money on a daughter's education because girls weren't supposed to waste their time that way. He expected your mother to get married, have babies, take care of house and home."

"Gramps doesn't seem all that old fashioned."

"Well, he's changed with the times, too. Maybe he even regrets it a little, not encouraging your mother to go on with her education. But see, he didn't have a college education himself. He didn't see a need for it. Gramps was a farmer, he'd been earning his living since he was just a kid himself, took over the family farm at sixteen when his own father died. College was one of those high-falutin' things that foreigners did, as far as Gramps was concerned.

Chapter 16

The first thing I saw out my window the next morning was Joe's truck parked in front of our house. He wore a big black cowboy hat and Orville rode shotgun. From my window it looked like the ape might be eating sunflower seeds. His lips would pucker as he spit them out the window. Joe's head was down like maybe he was reading a book or a magazine.

My cell phone started buzzing, another note from James.

did u get my note about tennyson? other books missing. filing police report today. please call. would like to have complete inventory of what is missing.

"I'm missing, you idiot." I fumed. Instead of deleting the message, I typed back.

I took Tennyson. Shakespeare. Bryant. Dickenson. In short, all books that were mine. Check my closet. It's empty, too. You haven't been robbed. I left you.

My finger hovered over the send key. I couldn't believe James still hadn't missed me. I wanted him to notice. I couldn't bring myself to make it easy for him.

"What'cha doing?" my brother's voice came from the doorway.

I moved my finger to the delete key. Delete, delete, delete, until the entire message was gone. Eventually James would be forced to call my parents' landline. Surely curiosity, my lack of response and lack of return, would eventually get the best of him.

"I'm going back out to look for the tiger," Zach said. "She was sighted up north by Hangman's Bridge."

"North? But she was almost 20 miles south when I saw her."

Zach shrugged his shoulders and grinned. "Just what I heard, farmer up north has tracks and everything. Should I tell Joe to wait?"

I looked out the window.

"I don't think there's room in that truck for you, me, Joe and Orville." Actually, I was thinking that I'd be well served keeping my face as far from Joe as possible. He was trouble, just like my dad said. And it didn't help that he knew about James.

I listened as Zach tore down the stairs. I got up and shuffled down the hallway to the bathroom. Mom came out of her room. "Is your brother gone?" she asked.

I wasn't sure if she wanted to catch him, or if she was waiting to show her face after he had already gone.

"He's gone with Joe," I said. "They're going up north of town to look for that white tiger."

Mom looked at me for a minute so sternly I thought she might carry on Zach's lecture from last night with me. "What do you think of your brother taking a gap year?" she demanded.

"I really have to go to the bathroom, Mom," I ducked my head and tried to scoot around her. She followed.

"Was this your idea? Did you put this gap year nonsense into his head?" she talked loudly through the bathroom door.

"No, Mom," I answered, hoping she would leave it alone.

The hallway remained quiet, so I assumed I was safe to leave the bathroom. Mom was standing in my room, however, looking out the window. "What on earth are they doing with that orangutan?" Mom asked.

Orville scampered back and forth across the lawn, acting like a real monkey for the first time since I'd met him, if you didn't count the shenanigans he pulled on stage at the graduation yesterday. He had a notebook tucked under one arm. Joe yelled and waved his hat. My brother stood in the back of the pickup truck laughing. Lisa watched the merriment cautiously from her yard. Orville grabbed Joe's hat and ran away on feet and knuckles, put the hat on his head and then slingshot himself around the light pole in our front yard.

Mom had one hand over her mouth. Zach whooped and clapped, then called to Orville like one might call a puppy. I heard the door to the house opening and my mother yelped.

"That animal will not come in my house," she roared, charging out of my room and down the stairs.

I went to the banister and looked down. A strip of orange fur went zip in one direction, my mother close behind. I dashed into my room to find my jeans and tennis shoes. Everything went quiet downstairs. I turned around to find Orville standing in my doorway. He had that composed look about him again, looking like a butler or chauffer, except for the fact that he was wearing a cowboy hat and breathing heavy.

"Get that animal out of my house," I heard my mother's voice from downstairs.

"Yes, Ma'am."

It had to be Joe.

"I'll get him, Mrs. Renzelmen."

"Hey Orville," I said, thinking about our last encounter when the ape had tried to throw me through the side of the truck. "What's up, Buddy?" I added, thinking I might charm him.

He flashed me his big ape grin, stuck his quivering lip out a bit, then batted his eyes and grinned at me again. Orville took the notebook from under his arm. It was a sketch pad.

"You draw, Orville?" I asked. The ape shielded his eyes with his hand like he was embarrassed by the thought.

I took the notebook he offered, and flipped it open to the first page. There was a line drawing of Orville himself, in Dodge City Sheriff's gear complete with gun and holster.

"Very nice," I said with admiration.

I turned to the next page which showed cattle in a field, a lone giraffe in the middle of the herd. There were a few close-up sketches of the giraffe, a drawing of an otter, then a group of otters wandering down a straight Kansas highway. The detail was stunning.

"Who drew these, Orville?" I asked. The ape launched himself forward, spun in a circle and started making rude hand gestures toward the door. Joe appeared.

"Just give it back, Orville," Joe said.

Orville flipped Joe the bird.

"Go ahead, be rude," Joe admonished. "I just want my book back."

"You drew these?" The question came out sounding more skeptical than I really felt. I remembered that Joe had spent a lot of time in art class in high school, though I'd always kind of imagined that was because he was lacking in facilities to take on more challenging classes, not that he might actually be a little on the advanced side, at least as far as art was concerned. "These are really good," I said, turning the page and examining a close up sketch of Orville looking thoughtful.

Joe stepped into the room and reached for the book. Orville put his long arms out. He'd have made an excellent guard in a basketball game. He stepped forward, toward Joe, as if protecting me.

I flipped another page. "What did you do to piss off Orville?" I asked Joe. "I thought he was your biggest fan."

Joe grinned, but kept his eyes on the ape. "Orville," he said with gritted teeth. "You're about to cross all my lines. I'm not letting you ride in my truck no more."

I was holding the sketchpad in my hands, but watching the standoff between Orville and Joe. My mother came into the room and was cautiously circling the ape. Orville seemed content to let her by, as long as Joe didn't move a muscle.

"Is this animal dangerous?" she whispered loudly. "I've called Doc Stueve. He's coming over with the tranquilizer gun and that gypsy girl."

At this, Orville swung his head around and glared at my mother. I thought for a moment that he was going to flip her the bird, as well, but he quickly returned his attention to Joe.

"Oh my, that's lovely," my mother said. I'd been watching Joe, whose ears immediately flamed red.

I looked down at the sketchbook in my hands to see a picture of myself. It was just my face and my eyes were filled with such sadness, I almost let out a sob right then and there.

Mom turned the page. The next image was me, as well the next. Scenes from our day together, hunting tigers. Me looking off into the distance, sitting in the truckbed with Orville's head on my lap.

I looked up at Joe, who had his hands shoved deep in his pockets. "Orville," he muttered. "You're not an ape, you're a rat.

Orville finally dropped his defensive pose and slouched up to Joe, planting a big slobbery kiss on his cheek.

"Joe?" Mom asked, "Is this your work? I had no idea you were an artist. These are absolutely stunning." We were looking at a page with a white tiger drawn. The following page showed profiles of me and the tigress together.

I felt my ears might be matching Joe's in color.

Mom didn't even seem to be registering the fact that most of the sketches were of me, a fact that left me feeling somewhere between uncomfortable and flattered. I wasn't the type of person to spend a lot of time thinking about my looks. I was pretty sure I wasn't actually this attractive, but there was no doubt that the person who drew these images found me attractive.

"Have you ever showed your work?" Mom asked Joe. "You should take it to the arts center. They would want to display it."

Joe had his arms crossed tight across his chest and a bit of a frown on his face. He didn't look embarrassed any more, just a wee bit angry.

Orville was hugging on Joe again, giving him big flirty eyes and a big ape grin.

"Now can I have my book back?" Joe asked Orville, avoiding eye contact with me.

Orville sidled up to Mom and me and politely plucked the book from our hands. He closed the cover, blew Mom a raspberry, and swaggered back to Joe.

"I'm sorry about the ape in your house, Ma'am," Joe said as he grabbed his book with both hands, holding on like he was afraid Orville would snatch it back again. "We'll be going now."

Zach stomped up the stairs. "Orville? Joe?" You guys coming?"

Mom watched in silence. I quickly finished putting on my tennis shoes and followed them out of the room.

"Where are you going?" Mom asked.

"I'm going tiger hunting," I yelled back at her.

Zach and Joe were already in the truck when I got out there. Orville was dallying. When the ape saw me, he stood up tall, throwing his arms in the air, the universal sign for victory.

"Thanks, Orville," I said, as the ape held open the little half door that led to the extended cab portion of Joe's truck."

Orville blew me a raspberry, then climbed in beside me and shut the door.

Chapter 17

Joe had a GPS in his truck that led us to a farmer's house near Jetmore. For the entire ride, we listened to the computer voice advise us we were on the wrong road, "recalculating... recalculating." The farmer, who introduced himself as Bob, seemed to be expecting us, but hesitated when he saw Orville. "You sure that ape's okay here? No chain? No leash or anything?"

"Orville's good," my brother answered. "He's more human than half of us."

Bob looked skeptical, but led us toward his barn anyway. "I just don't want you getting any ideas about my cattle," he finally turned and spoke to Orville who responded with a smile that showed all his teeth and batted his long eyelashes.

We followed Bob through the barn and out back to a stock tank that had been run over considerably if the mud surrounding it was any sign. "Here they are. There. There. And there."

Bob pointed out three prints that clearly belonged to a very large cat.

"You ever get cougars out here?" Joe asked.

"Hell, I hope not," Bob answered. "Not that big. That's your circus cat. She's out there somewhere," Bob gestured to the endless expanse of land surrounding us. "And so are my 80 head of cattle. I counted them this morning, and they were still all there. But if you all want that cat, somebody better find her before she starts treating my pasture like a buffet.

"Thanks, Bob." Joe answered. "You don't mind if we take vehicles out in your pasture?"

"Just don't go knocking down any fences," Bob answered gruffly. "There's a gate at every section on the west side along this fence line. You can get to everything, but if my fence is up, put it back up, and if it's down, leave it down. I rotate my cattle through here, you know. There's order to my madness. Just respect it, that's all I ask."

My brother was on his cell phone, talking to Doc Stueve, I assumed.

"Sure looks like a cat print to me," Zach was saying. "I don't know why she'd change direction. But I'm betting she's been here, and not too long ago either."

Joe walked slowly this way and that. Orville held his hand, following along happily. I wandered up beside them and Orville immediately began to pout.

"Make up your mind you stupid ape," I grumbled. Orville grinned and batted his eyes at me, then leaned into Joe and petted Joe's arm.

"See any more tracks?" I asked.

"Nah. It's so dry here. If he hadn't run that tank over, we'd have no idea she'd been here," Joe answered.

I looked out across the pastures. "Think she'd cross Bob's fences?"

"Sure," Joe answered. "She'd go right under some of those spots. He's got the top strung up tight and the electric wire, but he hasn't been worried about anything but a full grown steer getting out in years. Even a big tiger could squeeze right under."

Orville dropped to his belly and did a roll beneath the fence as if to demonstrate. He got up looking satisfied with himself.

"Hey," Bob yelled. "I'd appreciate it if you kept that ape with you. Don't let him go running off like that."

"You hear that, Orville?" Joe said, laughing. "Don't go running off."

Orville pulled himself up on the wooden post that the fence was tied to. He balanced neatly on one foot and put his arms up like a ballet dancer. The grace immediately ended when he leaped down between Joe and I, knuckle walked over to Bob and gave him a polite little wave. Then Orville stood up and sauntered back to us, took Joe's hand and kissed it. Even Bob was smiling by the time Orville finished his little performance.

Zach shoved his cell phone back into his pocket. "Why don't you two head on out? Orville and I will wait for Doc Stueve. Be in touch by phone?"

"You're probably going to lose cell phone service out there," Bob said.

"I've got the CB radio," said Joe. "If Doc brings the jeep, he'll have his too."

I hesitated, unsure if I wanted to be alone with Joe or not. Zach shooed me with a wave of his hand. "Rita coming with Doc?" I asked.

"I hope so," said Zach with a grin.

Joe and I climbed into the pickup truck and Orville squatted in the dirt, pouting. The ape pounded his hand on his head.

"You are such a drama queen," I shouted as Joe started up the truck and we lurched forward. Bob held the first gate open for us. Orville thumbed his nose at me.

"It's weird, isn't it?" Joe said after a few minutes of silence. We had both windows down. The wind rushing through the cab was hot and dry. I fished in my pocket for a ponytail holder and did my best to tie my hair up. I caught Joe watching me out of the corner of his eye.

"Hunting tiger in Kansas?" I asked. "Or your newest red-haired girlfriend?"

Joe shook his head and kind of laughed. "Don't be like that," he said.

"And what, exactly, is that?"

"Look, I know I was an ass in high school. I know I got a little full of myself and I dated a lot of girls, okay? But that's not me. That's not who I am now."

I thought about my dad's warning.

"You did date a lot of girls," I said. "Broke a lot of hearts, I suppose."

Joe shrugged. "Maybe," he said. "I hope not." After a long stretch of silence, he said, "You think I should try to make amends? Look them all up and tell them I'm sorry for being such a jerk?"

The truck jumped a couple of deep ruts. I pressed my feet to the floor to keep myself in place. "I don't know," I finally said. "For most of those girls, it was probably the highlight of their high school careers, dating you."

I noticed his ears flared a little pink again.

"I don't think of you that way," I said, feeling a bit soft for him. "I mean, you changed a lot in high school, but I always remembered you the way you were in our eighth grade home economics class. You were sweet. And kind of shy."

"I stuttered, and I couldn't look a girl in the eye when I talked to her," he said, shaking his head. "No thanks. It was easier being an ass."

"So what changed? What are you now?" I asked.

Joe slowed the truck, his eyes trained on the horizon. "Which way?" he asked.

I looked at our options, the cattle path to the right was worn fairly deep. "West," I said. "If I were her, I'd be traveling west."

I jumped out of the truck and unhooked the wire fence. I pulled it back far enough he could drive through and then hooked it tight again. When I got back in the truck, he said, "Joe. I'm just your average Joe."

We rode for miles and miles in silence, both of us following the horizon with our eyes. I had to get out twice more to open and close fences. The terrain was getting hillier. I knew were getting close to the area where crevices and old waterways marked the land. There were those who described the area we were approaching as canyons.

"So no more girl-of-the-week?" I asked.

Joe smiled. "I haven't been on a date in more than a year."

I laughed. "A year? What about Orville? He seems pretty sweet on you."

"That ape is nuts," Joe said, laughing.

"So why no dating? Is this a religious conversion or something?" That's about the time I spied the gas gauge on Joe's truck. "Your gauge broke?" I asked.

"Nah," Joe said before his jaw clinched. "Crap!" he said, pounding his hand on the steering wheel. "I was going to fill up after I picked up you and Zach. I completely forgot."

He stopped and pulled out his cell phone. The marker on the gauge showed well below empty. "Fumes," he said. "I'm running on fumes."

He got out of the truck and jumped into the bed, holding the cell phone high in the air for service. "Nothing," he declared.

I reached over and turned the volume up on the CB radio. "Doc and I are on the same frequency," Joe said. "He's about the only one I use this with anymore."

"10-4 Doc, this is Joe Bird, come in."

"Joe Bird?" I giggled.

Joe rolled his eyes at me and we listened to the static. He turned the key off and his truck stopped rumbling. "There's no way we'll make it back to Bob's. Crap," he said again.

I looked at him for a moment, then turned and pulled one of the tranquilizer guns from the rack in the back. "Well, we're hunting tiger, right?" I said, swinging open the door of Joe's truck. "Let's leave a note for Doc, and go on foot. We're close to the lake bed and the canyons," I said. "We'll be less likely to run her off on foot anyway."

Joe didn't hesitate. He pulled a notebook from his glove compartment and scribbled a note. He got out and stuck it under his windshield wiper, then got the second tranquilizer gun down from the rack. He pulled a pack from the back seat and slipped his arms in the straps.

We hiked in silence. I was glad for the constant breeze and the tall grass made me glad I'd worn jeans, as well.

"I don't suppose you have water in that pack?" I worked up the nerve to ask.

Joe smiled. "I was a Boy Scout. I come prepared." He pulled a canteen from the backpack and passed it to me. Then he pulled out a couple of granola bars. He walked to a little rise where the grass was fairly short, and kicked out a spot for us to sit on. We sat down, shoulder to shoulder and ate the granola bars, both of us watching and listening.

He took my wrapper and shoved it back in his pack. We headed toward the line of tall trees, sure sign of a river bed. As we approached, the ground dropped off and the prairie grass gave way to brush and thistle. I suddenly stopped when the ground beneath me turn sandy. "Look!" I whispered excitedly. There in front of us, clear as day, was an enormous cat print. Joe bent his head to the ground. Another, and then another, and then another.

"She's been here, alright," he whispered. We both craned our necks, looking in every direction. The ground grew grassy again and the clearly visible tracks disappeared.

"So Boy Scout, where's your tracking badge?" I asked.

Joe shrugged. "I can identify coyote poop," he offered.

Chapter 18

The sun was dropping low in the sky and Joe and I were seated in a dry river bed eating ham and cheese sandwiches and potato chips from a bag that sat between us. Joe pulled out his cell phone and glanced at it. "No bars," he said. Of course there wouldn't be any bars in this hole."

"She could be watching us right now," I said. The brush was thick in this area and a forest of small trees had taken over the riverbed. The hair on the back of my neck stood up. I looked at Joe to see if he might be getting the same inkling.

"Doc's never going to find us out here. If we're lucky, he's found the truck and my note. Maybe he'll have driven back to Bob's and brought us gas by now."

"Knowing Doc," I said. "He'll have a can of gas with him."

Joe nodded. "Doc was a good Boy Scout," he said. "You can count on Doc to always be prepared."

I finished the last bite of my sandwich and grabbed a big handful of chips from the bag. Joe pulled out a second canteen of water. We had already drunk the first dry.

"I like the way you aren't afraid to eat," Joe said. I turned to find him staring at me, his own half-eaten sandwich still in his hand. "So many girls, they don't really seem to enjoy their food. They'd have picked off the crust or complained that the ham was too warm or something."

"Well," I said, unsure where this was headed. "I was hungry. We've been riding forever today and then walking even longer than that. And…" I shrugged my shoulders. "Picnic sandwiches, the kind that get a little squished and over-warm in the bag while in route to your destination? Those sandwiches are the very best kind."

Joe smiled. "I'll buy you a coney dog at Sonic when we get out of here," he said.

"And tots with cheese?" I asked.

"Tots with cheese," he agreed. "And ice cream."

Deal," I held up my hand and he high-fived me.

He finished his sandwich and we watched the sun fall through the sky. "I don't suppose you have flashlights in that bag?" I asked. It occurred to me that we were going to be out here in the Kansas wild in the dark in less than thirty minutes.

Joe opened the back pack and pushed all of our trash back into it. He pulled out two flashlights, one red and one blue.

"We should head back to the truck," Joe said.

What I didn't count on was how spooky it would get when the sun went down. Joe just walked on, seemingly without a care in the world. I started thinking about the tigress, however. The idea of seeing her when it was daylight had given me a bit of a thrill, but when I thought of seeing her out here in the dark, my hair stood on end. The bearded lady had emphasized over and over again that she was a tame, circus tiger, but she hadn't exactly come when they called kitty, kitty.

I thought of my earlier encounter with her. It had been four days. What if she had been unsuccessful at catching her own food and was really hungry by now? What if she was tired and desperate or Joe and I just looked like easy pickings? What if she ran because she was tired of being in the circus and seeing people put her in the mood for revenge? I sped up, trying to stick as close to Joe as possible without actually bumping into him.

"Have you thought about what would happen if we ran into her in the dark?" I finally asked, feeling a bit winded from my effort to keep up.

Joe raised the tranquilizer gun and I saw that his finger was on the trigger. Maybe he had been thinking about the big cat too. The final glimmer of red from the setting sun escaped from the sky. Joe stopped suddenly and I ran, full body, into him.

"Shh," he hushed me when I started to apologize.

I froze in place, listening hard. The sounds of night closed in on us, the hoot of an owl, the scurry of something small along the ground, the song of a bull frog croaking over some distant puddle of water.

"What did you hear?" I finally asked in a whisper.

"I don't know," Joe said. "It was probably nothing."

He began walking again, this time at a much slower pace. He kept reaching his arm around behind as if to make sure that I was still there. I finally took his hand and we walked together, me swinging my light from the path in front of us and to the right, him swinging his light from the path in front of us and to the left.

After a bit he stopped again.

"Does any of this look familiar?" he asked.

I shone my light around us, full circle. "It all pretty much looks the same," I said.

Joe chuckled.

"What?" I asked, trying to sound calm and casual.

"I have no idea where the truck is," he said. "I don't know if we've passed it or if we've not gone far enough yet." He shone the light on his watch. "We've been walking back almost as long as we were walking away."

"Yeah, but you were walking really fast for a while there," I whispered.

"Was I?" he asked, and I felt his grip tighten on my hand. "There it is again?"

"What?" I repeated, trying not to sound at all panicked.

"That sound. Listen."

I held my breath and tried to open my ears, but my eyes were so busy scanning the path in front of my flashlight that my hearing seemed to be obstructed.

"Turn off your light!" Joe pulled hard at my arm.

"What? What? What?" I whisper-screeched. To hell with the appearance of calm, I thought. If it was the tiger, it was like we were lighting up the menu.

Then I heard it. Crack, crack, crash. Something big was moving through the brush from the direction we had come. Maybe she'd been following us all along. Maybe that's why the hair had been standing up on the back of my neck. The reptile portion of my brain somehow knew that we were being stalked.

I fumbled with the safety on my tranquilizer gun one handed. I pulled my hand away from Joe, shouting at him to let go as I saw a flash of white up ahead. Crack, snap, crash. It was a large body moving quickly toward us. I felt Joe shove at me, perhaps hoping she would target him rather than me. I tripped and went down hard, unable to catch myself with my hands as I was struggling to keep the tranquilizer aimed in the direction the tiger was coming from. I felt the gun go off, and from the blur of white coming through the weeds, I was pretty sure I'd missed my target.

A roar rang out, however. It was loud and if any hairs on my head were standing on end before, it was nothing like they were now.

Goosebumps on top of goosebumps rose. I tasted blood in my mouth. Quickly, I rolled over and was on my hands and knees, searching for the flashlight.

The blur of white was still coming toward us. I couldn't see or hear Joe and decided the tiger was coming after me.

"Who goes there?" a voice shouted. It was a woman's voice. An oddly deep voice.

"Zelda?" I said, my voice trembling. I finally found the flashlight and punched the button, illuminating the spot where I'd last spotted the white blur.

The bearded lady held her hand up against the blinding glare of my spotlight. She cursed me. "Point that damned thing the other way," she shouted.

I swung the light off her face. "What are you doing out here?" I asked, feeling breathless and a bit lightheaded. I tasted blood where I must have bit my lip.

"I'm looking for my tiger," she said matter-of-factly. "What are you doing out here?"

She kept looking to the spot where my light was resting. I watched her, wondering why anyone would go on a tiger hunt dressed all in white, from head to toe. Even her head was covered with some kind of white silk scarf.

"We're looking for the tiger, too."

"Hmm... that's what you call this?" she asked.

"Well, it got dark and, we might have gotten a little bit lost," I was trying to think how to explain. Surely the bearded lady's presence meant Doc Stueve was near also. I hoped he had found Joe's truck and taken care of our gas problem.

The bearded lady just looked at me. "Look," she finally said. "I don't know what kind of perverted games you are into lady, but I don't think it's a good idea to leave him here like this. My tiger comes along, she just might start snacking on him. Not that she's a people eater, but she's been out a while. It's hard telling what would tempt her."

The bearded lady brushed past me. "Doc's got the jeep parked up this hill."

I let my flashlight stray up the path ahead of her. I could see the reflection off Doc's red jeep in the distance. I sighed. "At least we're close," I said. "Joe?"

I turned back around, shining my light like a beacon. I couldn't see Joe anywhere.

"Joe?" I called again. "Not funny, Joe. Where the hell are you?"

That's when my beam of light fell on the bottom of Joe's tennis shoes. "Joe?" I whispered. I let my flashlight travel up his leg. He was lying in weeds so tall that his entire body was pretty much hidden from sight. I stepped closer until I could see his entire figure, prone on the ground. There in the back of his thigh was the red tassel of the tranquilizer dart.

Joe was sleeping soundly, face down on the ground.

Chapter 19

Doc Stueve couldn't stop laughing. It took the Doc, my brother, Rita and me to get Joe lifted and into the back of Joe's truck. Zach unzipped a sleeping bag and we rolled Joe onto it.

"Are you sure he's going to be okay?" I asked Doc.

"Well," Doc answered. "I had that tranq loaded for a 300 pound tiger. It's a little more than I would have prescribed for Joe here, but I think he'll come out of it okay." He laughed some more, shushing long enough to check Joe's pulse again before breaking into another cackle of glee.

The bearded lady stood off in the distance, judging me from afar.

"I'm so sorry, Joe," I whispered, wishing I had at least managed to down the bearded lady instead.

"Really, he'll be fine," Doc said.

Rita put her hand on my shoulder. "It'll be okay," she said, her voice melodic. I glanced up at my brother. He hadn't said much, but I could see in the light of Doc's lantern that he was pretty well stuck in Rita's mire. He couldn't take his eyes off of her, and he had a kind of distant, not really tuned-in with the rest of us look about him.

"It'll be fine Jen," he finally said, as if noticing me for the first time. I couldn't remember him ever call me just Jen before. Was his childhood nickname for me too immature for his new infatuation?

Doc had already poured a gallon of gas that he carried as a spare into Joe's truck and assured me that in the morning he would follow us out of Bob's pasture and make sure we made it to the nearest station in Jetmore. He pulled a cooler out of the back of his jeep. I could hear the melted ice slosh around as he put it on the ground.

"Build a fire in the camp stove," he instructed Zach. "I've got hot dogs, buns, and beer. That'll do for everyone. Not counting Joe." Doc tipped his head back and let out another howl of laughter.

Orville seemingly came from nowhere. He knuckle walked up to the truck and stood there looking from me to Rita to Joe. He finally pulled himself into the back of the truck and started inspecting the sleeping figure of his favorite man. He ran his big ape finger along Joe's arm, jarring him a little as if testing to see if he would wake up.

"Gentle, Orville," Rita commanded. "Joe's asleep. He's a very tired Joe. We need to leave him be."

Orville seemed to accept this, and scooted himself into the corner of the truck, leaning his head back and staring up at the night sky.

I took one last look at Joe in the light of Doc Stueve's lantern and slid out of the bed of the truck. Zach brought me a beer from the cooler. He had one in his hand for Rita, as well. She thanked him and gave a little twirl, though she wasn't wearing a flowing long skirt today. Just blue jeans rolled up almost to her knees. But she was still colorful with a scarf tied around her long hair, holding it back in a ponytail that turned into a braid.

Rita offered her assistance to Doc and I put my hand on my brother's arm, holding him back so that I could talk to him.

"No sign of the tiger?" I asked.

"Nah. You all?"

"We found more tracks. She's definitely been around here."

Zach and I both turned our backs on the impromptu camp and looked out into the darkness. The stars twinkled above us. We listened to the darkness for a moment, then music started playing. Rita had gotten out a guitar and was strumming in the darkness.

"She's fantastic, isn't she," Zach seemed to be making a statement more than asking a question.

"She seems really nice," I agreed. "But..."

"Oh god. Don't even start. You're my sister. You can't take their side," he said.

"I'm not," I defended myself. But I was, I realized just as quickly.

"You know, not going to college isn't about Rita," Zach said. "I've been thinking about this for a long time. I don't know what I want to do with my life. Why waste a year preparing for vet school when I might go an entirely different direction? What if I just went with computers? I have a friend... an online friend... who is testing games in Austin. He says he could get me a job, Jen-Jen. I could go work and make some money and maybe decide if gaming, computers, is where my passion is."

"You'd better call it computers if you want to sell it to Mom and Dad," I advised.

"Don't I know it," Zach laughed. "Mom would have a cow if she thought I was considering a career playing video games." Zach gave exaggerated air quotes when he said the word, career.

"It's normal, right?" A kind of pleading quality had crept into his voice. "I mean, I just graduated from high school. How am I supposed to know what I want to do with my life?"

I thought about his question. Why hadn't I ever asked it? Why had I just assumed that doing what other people suggested I do was enough?

Rita started singing along as she played. Doc Stueve joined in, and even the bearded lady seemed to be drawn closer by Rita's melody.

"Wow," I said. "She's really good."

Rita sang *Blackbird*, a song by the Beatles that Zach and I both knew because our parents were huge fans. Zach started back toward the jeep, but I stopped him. He turned to look at me.

"You're completely normal, Zach," I said. "You're normal, and I think you're right not to go straight to college."

My little brother smiled at me and for a moment I felt like a true big sister again, little brother's comforter and keeper. I wrapped my arms around him and he squeezed me in a big old bear hug, lifting my feet from the ground. When he let me down he said, "I can't believe you tranquilized Joe."

We both laughed, but I headed for the truck and crawled up beside Joe to check his pulse, just to assure myself, again, that he would be okay. Orville watched me with gentle eyes that appeared to be getting sleepy. No pout. No defensive posturing. It was as if Orville was actually allowing that maybe I could have a little interest in Joe, as well.

"Thanks, Orville." I slid quietly out of the truck again, drawn to listen to Rita's singing. "You keep an eye on him," I instructed the ape.

Chapter 20

Orville's hairy chest was the first thing I saw the next morning as the sun broke on the horizon. He smelled like ape and I was hard pressed to imagine, for a moment, how I'd ended up in the clutches of an orangutan. He was snoring gently and so was the body on my other side. I turned my head just enough to see that it was Joe, still flat on his back, sleeping as soundly as he had apparently been since I hit him with the tranquilizer dart last evening. I pushed Orville's long monkey arm off of me and sat up. It was a little chilly, which hopefully explained the clinch the three of us had arrived at; I was pretty certain the couple of beers I'd had last night were not responsible.

I turned briefly to check Joe's pulse again, though his light snoring was more than enough to assure me he was still breathing.

I pulled myself up and stood. There was a haze over the land that was quickly dissipating with the rising sun. I could feel the night chill leave the air as breeze was buoyed and dried by the rising sun. Orville rolled to his feet and stood beside me. I had a picture of myself all of a sudden, standing on the open prairie with an ape at my side. Orville put his arm on my shoulder and grinned at me, as if imagining himself here with a human female was just as amusing to him.

The morning was alive with the sounds of birds chirping and insects making a ruckus. I closed my eyes and felt the breeze on my cheeks, listening to the wind and the thousand sounds of nature that bounced along it. Then that sound came again. For the second time in my life, I heard a tiger's roar. Not a caged tiger in the zoo, but the sound of a wild animal, roaming free. I felt the goosebumps rise on my arms, but I didn't feel afraid this time. She was out there. She was simply saying good morning. Letting us know she knew we were out here, as well. Why she hadn't come home to the circus, or to the people who so obviously cared for her, I couldn't imagine.

Sometimes a girl just knows when it's time to free herself, I supposed.

The door to the jeep flew open and Doc Stueve stumbled out, pulling a t-shirt over his head. Rita rose from the grass, a short distance away from the truck. I looked for my brother, and he appeared too, far enough away from Rita that it didn't seem as if they'd spent the night together, just happened to unroll sleeping bags in near proximity. Zach picked up the sleeping bag and sloppily rolled it beneath his arm. Rita picked up a blanket and shook it on the breeze, then collected her guitar and headed toward Doc's jeep. We were all scanning the horizon, waiting to hear the tiger's roar again.

"By golly," Doc breathed, stomping through the grass toward Orville and I. "She's really out there. I was beginning to think she was a figment of folk's imaginations."

He jumped into the back of the truck and inspected Joe. Orville and I were silent as we watched him take Joe's pulse. Doc looked long and hard at his watch. "He's doing fine," Doc said. "I wish I could say that he's going to feel well rested when this is over, but my guess is that he's going to have one hell of a hangover when he wakes up."

I cringed, watching Doc as he worked to keep the grin off his face. "Don't feel bad," Doc said. "There are a dozen girls in Dodge City who are singing your praises right now."

The hum of an airplane filled the air. I spotted the low-wing, homebuilt Vans in the distance. It seemed to be headed right for us.

"That'll be Mike," said Doc. "He's going to be our spotter from the air again today."

Doc jogged back to his jeep and Orville and I followed. He opened the passenger door and pulled out his CB Radio. "Come in, Mike in the Sky, this is Doc. Over."

"This is Mike in the Sky, You're coming in loud and clear, Doc. Over."

"You've come to the right place at the right time, Mike. We just heard her. She's here. She's here and she's very, very close. Over."

The hum of the plane grew louder.

"I have eyes on you, Doc. Should I follow the river bed? Over."

We all watched, our heads tipping back as the plane grew large overhead. It roared over us and then Mike banked and turned in a tight curve. He was so close we could see his grinning face through the side of the cockpit window.

We all waved, but Orville waved biggest. He blew raspberries at the plane and skipped along on his knuckles for a few paces, overjoyed.

"The river bed, yes. That's the direction she came from. I'd be surprised if she were more than a quarter mile away. Over."

The plane banked again and flew away from us, in the direction the bearded lady had gone.

"We just looking for tiger?" Mike's voice came over the radio along with some static. "Cause I've got one fine circus freak here. Over." He laughed.

Doc shook his head and kind of looked toward Rita, who was walking toward us with my brother, Zach. "Just the tiger, Mike," Doc said. "Eyes out for the tiger. Over."

Orville rushed to Rita and Zach, inserting himself between them like a small child. He dropped his upright posture for more of a lumbering monkey walk, taking turns holding on to Zach with his left hand and then Rita with his right.

We all gathered and watched as the small plane followed the river, banked and turned, then followed the river in the other direction. Each time the plane banked and turned, Mike flew a little further away before coming back again. He flew along the near bank of the empty river bed and then the far bank of the empty river bed. Orville got tired of standing and sat down. Rita made her way back to the pickup truck and sat on the tail gate. I followed.

"Man, he's out big time," she said, indicating Joe who didn't even twitch at the roaring sound of the plane overhead. I watched his chest to make sure it was still rising and falling.

"You don't think this could cause brain damage or anything?" I asked.

Rita shrugged. "If Doc's not worried, I wouldn't be worried," she said.

"What if Doc's not telling me he's worried, because he doesn't want me to feel bad?"

"Well, if Doc was really worried, he'd have taken him on in to Dodge this morning, right? Get him checked out by a hospital or something?"

The sound of the plane was increasing in volume again. Rita and I were quiet as we watched it fly by. The body in the back of the truck moaned, and we both quickly turned to look at Joe. He wasn't moving, however. Just breathing the same, deep-sleep breathing he'd been doing since I shot him.

Mike started flying in a spiral, starting with a tight circle that he let grow bigger and bigger. I could see that Doc Stueve was talking into the radio again.

"Poor Lucy," Rita said. "It must be frightening for her, being out there all alone."

"Lucy?" I asked. I'd never heard the big cat referred to as anything other than the Mingleeng White Tiger or the Tigress.

"It's my name for her. Everyone at the circus just refers to her as the Tigress. I felt she needed a name. I call her Lucy."

Do you know how they get white tigers?" Rita asked.

"No," I answered. "How do they get white tigers?"

"It's quite horrible, really." Rita's voice continued to slip in and out of accent. Sometimes she sounded regal, almost royal. I could imagine her a real gypsy princess. Other times she just sounded like a girl from Texas, or maybe even deeper south. "White tigers can only be born when siblings are interbred. They take tigers from a line where the white gene is known to exist, and then breed sibling pairs until a white tiger results."

"That's a bit creepy," I admitted, thinking Rita may have just ruined the allure of the white tiger for me for good.

"It gets worse," Rita said. "The coloring is the result of a recessive gene trait."

"Thus the sibling parents," I say, "Increasing the odds that the recessive gene is passed through each parent."

"Yes, but with the coloring typically comes a whole host of other problems," said Rita. "Something like only 1 in 10 white tigers ever born in captivity even lives to be shown in a circus or zoo. Most of them die of other health complications, or they end up so deformed that it would be impossible to show them to the public."

"Eww," I grimaced. "That's terrible."

"It's beyond terrible," Rita said. "It's the most inhumane, horrific violation of nature."

I looked at Rita, who had tears in her eyes. "People are terrible creatures, sometimes," she whispered.

Joe began to come out of his trance about mid-morning. He was anything but lucid, but he started to flinch when someone made a loud noise near him and would respond with mumbling when we talked directly to him. It was as if there was a conscious Joe deep inside his body that was really struggling to surface.

"I'm so sorry, Joe," I mumbled when the others took off for another short hike into the riverbed to look for Lucy the Tigress again. Doc had hoped the sound of the plane would push her into the open, but she remained out of sight. They decided to look for shelter and cave like entrances where she might hide. Mike returned to the Dodge City airport to refuel.

I thought that maybe by apologizing to Joe before he completely became conscious, I could relieve some of my guilt without having to totally degrade myself in front of him.

"Ouch," was the first intelligible word that came from Joe's mouth.

"Hey, Joe," I said, wishing Rita or Doc were here to back me up when he finally awoke.

But Joe didn't answer. His eyes remained closed and his breathing steady. I eventually stopped watching Joe to watch the horizon again. I kept imagining Rita coming up out of the river bed with Lucy at her heels, the two of them crossing the land majestically, Rita in white flowing skirts adorned with colorful scarves and bangle bracelets, and the blue-eyed Lucy, an extra-large kitty cat at her heels.

I thought about what Rita told me, about the horror of a white tiger's origins, and how the story had moved Rita to tears. I wondered about Rita's own backstory and wondered if my brother were mature enough for a girl who came with such obvious scars.

"You shouldn't underestimate your little brother," Joe's voice startled me.

"Wha... Did I?"

"You just said, 'Is my brother mature enough for a girl who comes with so many scars. You said that out loud.'"

I turned to look at Joe and he was lying with one arm thrown up over his eyes, shielding himself from the sun.

"Good morning, Joe," I finally said, getting over my surprise at his surfacing.

"What the hell?" he asked. I thought for a moment that he was going to roll forward to sit up, but his face contorted with pain and he just stayed there, unmoving. "Am I paralyzed?" he finally asked.

I looked at his arm, raised to shield his eyes. "You seem to have use of at least your right arm," I said, offering no more explanation than that.

"My head," he moaned. "I feel like my head might just explode if I move. And my back. Jesus, my back is aching."

"You're okay, Joe. Just a little sore," I offered. "Doc says you'll be just fine."

"Doc? What the hell? Am I in a hospital?" he raised his right arm and searched the sky with his eyes. "Am I dead?"

I swallowed hard. "What do you remember, Joe?" I asked.

"I remember…" his voice trailed off, as if he suddenly realized his memory was void and blank or if what he was remembering was untrustworthy.

"We watched the sunset," he finally offered.

"I gave you the blue flashlight," he added after a few minutes.

"The tiger," his voice rose an octave or two. "Oh shit! The tiger. Did the tiger eat me?" he gasped, pulling himself to a sitting position and grasping at his arms and legs with his fingers as if testing everything to make sure everything was still there."

"No, no," I shushed him. "We never found the tiger. It was the bearded lady that was coming through the brush at us."

"The bearded lady?" he asked, confused. "What? Did she hit me with a truck?"

I couldn't help but laugh a little.

"It wasn't her, Joe. It was me."

"You hit me with a truck?" he asked.

"I hit you with the tranquilizer dart. I stumbled. You kind of pushed me out of the way. I think you were trying to save me from the tiger… well, the bearded lady. But we both thought she was the tiger."

"You shot me?" he said, his tone gaining some lucidity.

"Accidentally," I said. "You pushed me and I stumbled and the gun went off."

"I remember the tiger coming through the brush," he said.

"And the dart hit you in the thigh." I touched him where the dart had pierced his blue jeans. He yelped.

"I'm sorry, Joe," I said, blushing, and trying not to laugh. His face was such a mixture of confusion and pain.

"So what happened to the tiger? Did we get her?"

"It wasn't the tiger. It was the bearded lady," I explained.

Joe looked around, orienting himself to time and place. "Where is everybody else?" he asked.

"Out looking for her again. The plane has been up all morning. Now they are re-checking the river bed, looking for any areas she might have been able to hide in. Would you like me to take you home?"

Joe was holding his head. He tried to shake it a few times, but it was obvious his headache was severe.

"What a minute," he finally said, peering at me seriously. "Did you say you shot me with the tranquilizer gun? Are you saying I've been knocked out with enough drug to bring down a 300 pound tiger?"

Chapter 21

I drove Joe's truck back to Jetmore where I filled the tank to the top on my own credit card. I tried not to think about how I might pay off the credit card. I didn't even have a job at the moment. That fact would really start to sting if I gave myself a moment to think about it.

Perhaps, I thought to myself, since James still didn't understand I'd left him, he'd just pay my credit card bill right along with his own. Technically, we kept separate bank accounts, but James was a bit compulsive about keeping bills paid and it was not unusual for him to bring the mail directly in and write checks for everything that had arrived that day. I used to try to pay him back every time he took care of a bill that was mine, but he would always shrug it off as if it were no big deal and, since he continued to "accidentally" pay my bills now and then, I decided maybe he saw it as a kind of a gift to me.

Maybe this one would slip through on James's dime, I thought with satisfaction. I fingered the card in my wallet. Maybe I should go charge up a whole lot more and see how far I could ride this horse.

Joe was dozing again in the seat beside me. I thought he'd probably be a horrible side-seat driver if all his faculties were clear, so I was thankful for his sleepy state. I pulled out onto the highway after filling up with gas and we went a couple of miles before Joe's eyes flew open and he lurched forward.

"I'm going to be sick," he said through clinched teeth. "Stop the truck! I'm going to be sick!"

I swerved off the road and applied the brakes. He had the door open before I'd rolled to a stop. He was heaving and clawing at his belt with his hands. I helped him undo it, and he rolled from the truck out onto the ground. I watched as he heaved until his stomach was empty on his hands and knees there upon the ground. I got out and went around the truck to see if I could help him.

"I can't believe you shot me," he was mumbling as I helped him to his feet. He was swaying and extremely unsteady. He'd gotten kind of clammy and his pulse was racing. I wished we had stayed with Doc, who could assure me that this was okay and that everything that was happening to Joe was normal for a guy who'd spent the last 16 hours in la-la land.

"I know, Joe. I'm so sorry." I had to really shove to get him back into the truck. Then I went back around to the driver's side and had to almost crawl back over him to get his seatbelt secured. When I got him all settled, half way in a seated position, I pulled back and looked at him. He was watching me. His eyes were a bit cloudy and bloodshot. In spite of everything, he smiled at me, a little half grin.

As we approached Dodge City, I debated the merits of taking him to his home versus my own. I was a little freaked out about the idea of leaving him alone. His color didn't look at all good and I kept picturing him suffering heart failure or something equally as horrible.

"Maybe I should take you to the hospital," I said. "Just to get you checked out."

It was a moment before Joe responded. "Nah. I'm all right. Just take me home."

"I don't think I should leave you alone," I said.

"You can stay," he said. "I'm just going to be sleeping, but whatever. You shot me. You might as well nurse me back to health." His eyes closed and I thought for a moment that he had gone back to sleep.

"I'm... I'm a little afraid to be with you alone," I admitted. "How about I take you back to my place?"

"Nah," Joe answered. "Doc said I was okay. I'll be okay."

"Doc is a veterinarian, not a people doctor," I reminded him.

Joe didn't say anything more and I made up my mind. I pulled out my cell phone, thinking I'd call home and give Mom and Dad a head's up. I changed my mind, remembering Dad's warning about Joe.

I shoved my phone in my pocket and just drove home. I pulled Joe's truck into the driveway, killed the motor, and jumped out. He seemed to be sleeping soundly again. It took a few shakes of his arm before I got him to open his eyes again. "We home?" he asked.

"Yep. We're here." He was so out of it I thought there was a good chance he wouldn't notice which house we had arrived at.

Joe slid out of the truck seat easily enough. He lifted one knee and then the other, but forward momentum seemed to be lacking. I bent until I got one of his arms around my shoulder. "Let's go, Joe."

"Let's go," he repeated. "Let's go, Joe."

He was heavier than I imagined and about every third step he would lean so heavily I was afraid I was actually going to collapse.

"Hey," Joe said with a slur. "You're very poetical. Let's go, Joe." He was starting to sound like a bad drunk. Just what I needed my dad to see. Me dragging Joe into the house acting three sheets to the wind in the middle of the day on a Tuesday.

"Jeni?" Mom was at the door, her voice was stern. "What? Where have you been? Why haven't you been answering your phone?"

She wasn't opening the screen door, and it occurred to me that she looked as if she might not let us in.

"What's wrong with him? Why have you brought him here? And where on earth is your brother?"

"It's okay, Mom. I'll tell you everything," I said. "Just let us in please. He's... sick. He just needs to rest and I didn't want to leave him alone."

Dad appeared in the doorway, as well. He pushed past my mother and caught Joe under the other arm. Joe's head kind of lolled as the bulk of his weight was pulled onto my father.

"Thanks, Dad," I said breathlessly. "He's okay, really. It's not his fault."

I kind of stumbled in the house behind my father and Joe, feeling rather extraneous at that point. "We've been north, out by Jetmore. The tiger's tracks have been seen out there. So we were looking for her, and..."

Dad was pushing Joe onto the couch because he'd kind of fallen forward and almost hit the floor when Dad first let go of him.

"She shot me," Joe's voice came out loud and clear. "Your daughter shot me, sir."

I turned to find my parents both staring at me, open mouthed. There was a third set of eyes looking at me, as well. Across from the couch, seated on my mom's delicate Queen Anne chair, was James, holding a cup of tea with his pinky finger lifted nearly as high as his eyebrows.

"I'm sorry," my mother said. "Did he just say that you shot him?"

Dad had taken his eyes off of me and seemed to be checking Joe over for bullet wounds.

"Not shot. Not like with a gun," I was having trouble making my voice loud enough to be heard. I was so blown away by James's presence here in my parents' living room. How long had he been here? What had they said to him? What had he said to them?

"It's okay," Joe was mumbling now. "Your daughter shot me, but it's okay. She didn't mean to."

Dad kneeled down in front of Joe. "We should get him to a doctor," he said to me, his voice stern.

"It's not like that Dad. It was the tranquilizer gun. The one we had for the tiger. I tripped. It went off. The tranquilizer dart hit Joe in the thigh."

"He's okay?" Dad asked, not looking at all convinced.

"I'm okay, Sir," Joe slurred. "And in spite of everything, even though she didn't call me after graduation, and she never visited or anything... even though she shot me, I'm still crazy mad in love with your daughter, Sir."

It was my turn to gape like a fish out of water.

I met my mother's eyes, then dad's, but I could only look at the cup of tea in James's hand.

"He's been drugged," I finally said. "Some really heavy drugs. He's... hallucinating. I'm not even sure he knows that it's me who shot him, who brought him home."

"Jeni Renzelmen," Joe moaned dreamily. "I've never gotten over you, Jeni Renzelmen."

If another tranquilizer dart had been available, I would have jammed it in his other thigh right then and there. I contemplated putting a pillow over his face. Instead, I leaned over and whispered harshly. "Just. Shut. Up."

His eyes opened just a crack. It took a moment for him to focus on my face. When he did, that half grin came back. "Hey, Jeni," he mumbled.

"Just shut up, Joe," I repeated. "Sleep."

This command seemed to have some effect on him. He pulled his arms up across his chest and hugged himself. Mom pulled the afghan off the back of the couch and covered him. Dad took a pillow and arranged it under Joe's head.

"Maybe..." My mom's face registered at least a half dozen emotions.

She started again in a whisper. "Perhaps we should move to the kitchen to let Joe sleep?" It was strange to see her without the words to express herself. It was strange to hear my Mom speak in questions rather than answers.

"Or, we'll go to the kitchen," my dad said, taking her arm. "I think Jeni and James might want to take a walk."

James was still sitting there with his cup raised, his pinky finger twitching. He put the cup down, stood and smoothed the front of his khaki slacks. He shook his head in agreement.

"Wonderful weather for a walk," he said lamely. He shoved his hands in his jacket pockets and headed for the door. He stepped out without so much as a look back to see if I was following.

"Mom. Dad. Really, this isn't what it looks like."

"You've been out with this guy all night," my father said through clenched teeth. "You barely know him."

"Where's your brother?" Mom demanded. Perhaps I was a lost cause, but she still saw a way to save my brother. "Is he with that circus girl? Is he…" Her voice caught and I was surprised to see tears roll down her cheeks. "What is happening?" she said to my father. "We were good parents. Where did we go wrong?"

All of a sudden, it wasn't shame or embarrassment that I felt, but anger. It boiled up in me as if I had been storing it in my gut all along, and had only, just now, released the valve. "Where did you go wrong?" I asked, my voice measured the first time. "Where did *you* go wrong?"

Mom looked at me, her eyes big and wide, lashes batting at tears that seemed ready to spill over.

"Did you ever stop to think, Mom, that this isn't about you? It's about me! Your daughter. I'm the one in pain here. I'm trying to figure out which end is up, and where the hell *I* went wrong. Did you ever stop to think that if you'd let me figure things out for myself in the first place, I might not be in this mess?"

My dad started to speak, but I cut him off.

"I came home because I thought this was a safe place to go. I thought that this is where I'd be able to figure out where I went wrong to begin with."

Mom swallowed and looked down at her feet. "Of course this is a safe place…"

"If you'll excuse me," I shouted. "I have something rather pressing to attend to right now. I have a lover to dump."

Tiger Hunting

James was the last person I wanted to see, of course, but I knew he'd be waiting somewhere outside that door, and until I'd corrected this one wrong in my life, I figured letting him dangle around my neck like an albatross would just slow me down on all the others.

He was standing by the rose bushes at the edge of the house, smoking a cigarette.

"Why are you here?" I asked, taking pleasure to see him startle and fling the cigarette to the ground. He stomped it into the green grass with his toe.

"I... You... Are you really leaving me?" he finally asked.

"I think I've made that quite clear," I answered.

As he stood there looking at me, it occurred to me that this really might be a blow to his huge ego. James wasn't used to being dumped.

"I don't share my vanity space. I don't share my closet space. I don't share my bed. Okay? You've got another girl coming round, fine. You have fun with her. But I don't share, and I shouldn't have shared with the first one. The one that was there before me. I screwed up. I'm done screwing up. I've already emptied the apartment of all my stuff. You can go home now. Are we clear?"

I turned, my arms crossed tight across my chest, and started to walk away.

"Brandy," he said. "Her name is Brandy, and it's not... It's not like that."

I stopped in spite of the little voice in my head telling me to just move on.

"Yes, I brought her home... I brought her into our apartment a couple of times while you were working, but then..." He actually looked ashamed of himself. It was worth standing there, watching his face without his typical look of smug superiority. "She's the one," he finally said. "She's the one I think I am meant to spend my life with, and I want to... undo this thing between you and I correctly, so that I can do something right in my life for once."

So maybe it wasn't shame I was seeing on his face. Smug bastard.

"I know this sounds stupid, and maybe I should have just let you walk away when I found your note..."

"So you did find the note?" I interjected.

"Just yesterday. I was cleaning off the table, looking for a bill."

"And that was your first clue? That note, five days after I've emptied all my belongings from the apartment, is the first clue you had that I was gone."

"I suppose not," he said, shoving his hands deeper into his pockets.

I found myself walking back toward him, loosening my arms from across my chest, sensing his vulnerability and wishing so badly that I could stop myself from responding to it.

"You wrote this paper when you were taking my class," he said. "I can't say that I ever really noticed you until you wrote that paper. It was the one titled, "Aspects of Fragmentation of Self." The one where you wrote about the series of selves a person becomes to explain the past, cope with the present, and prepare for the future. I read that paper and I thought, here is someone with a real voice. Here is someone who's not just pretending, not just putting on airs, but has a real voice and something to say to the world. I couldn't sleep that night I first read your paper. I kept trying to picture you, the girl in the far left row, second seat from the front. I knew that from the seating chart in my gradebook."

"The seat of invisibility," I said.

He looked surprised when I said this.

"It was my favorite place to sit in class. Close enough to be in on the discussion, if there was ever opportunity, yet not the center of attention," I explained.

"You wanted to be invisible?" he asked.

"Not exactly," I answered. Then I thought about it. "Maybe."

He sighed thoughtfully. "I've spent my whole life desiring to be seen," he said. "I've always had this idea that just around the corner, just the next step in my career, the next thing I would write, that would be the place where people finally noticed me."

"Are you kidding me?" I answered, thinking of all the parties we'd attended where he'd been right in the thick of things. Everyone always calling his name, asking him to sit at the head table. How many times had I been shuffled off to sit on my own at parties because James was so in demand as a most honored guest.

"You showed me your voice in that paper. I wanted to know you because I wanted to understand how someone so young could have such conviction, such broad understanding of the world, such confidence when using her own voice."

I shook my head at him. "And then you discovered it was a fluke."

He watched me, our eyes meeting for the longest I could ever remember since probably our very first date.

"I have to know," he said. "Did I break you?"

"What?" I sneered.

"Is it my fault you stopped writing? I mean, I've seen evidence all over the apartment. I know your voice is still there. The napkins you jot notes on. That story you had tucked in the book of Tennyson poems. When I first saw that piece of paper yesterday, when I was changing the sheets on the bed, at first I thought it was another one of your inspirations."

"Inspirations?"

"You know, your notes to yourself. About things you were going to write."

"I have no idea what you are talking about," I pictured myself pulling the pen out of my back pocket, where I always carried it. I did have a habit of writing thoughts down on scraps of paper. Napkins, corners of cardboard at the warehouse where I worked. It was my way of clearing my mind. An idea would be eating at me and I'd write it down, emptying it from my head. Then I could move forward. Go on to work the next thought for a while.

"I always thought that when you finally published whatever it was you were working on, all my efforts at becoming visible were going to come crashing down around me. It was like a ticking time clock, being with you. Just waiting for your shadow to overtake me."

I blinked and stared at him. "Are you high?" I finally asked.

"It is my fault then. I'm so sorry, Jennifer. I never meant to hold you back. I never meant to make you smaller or less. I need you to believe that. I need to make things right with you before I can move on."

I slid down against the wall of the house until my butt was resting on the edge of the porch. I tried to digest what James was saying to me. It made no sense. I had not given this man that much power over my life. I had not surrendered my voice for his companionship. Or had I?

"I don't remember that paper," I said. "I remember having to write something about *The Waste Land*, by T.S. Eliott. I remember the very act of reading *The Waste Land* was so exhausting, and the idea of having to interpret it and write about it so intimidating. So I finally just started taking it apart, line by line. I only wrote about the parts that made sense to me. I couldn't seem to grasp the big picture, so I just started writing about the little pieces and when I was done, I wasn't even sure what I had said."

James had come closer to me and was now perched on the edge of the concrete porch, as well.

"You didn't break anything in me, James," I finally said. "I don't know what you saw in that paper, but I was with you exactly what I was before you. Just someone too timid to find her own way in the world. Someone who had been counting on the good grace and good advice of those around her for years. You were just one more person I looked to for direction."

James watched me closely. He got up and walked across the yard to his car. He went around to the passenger side and opened up the door. When he stood up, he was holding what looked like a large metal cookie tin. I recognized it as a Christmas gift he had gotten from someone in the English department last year.

"You didn't take everything with you when you left," he said, coming back across the yard.

I didn't take the tin he was offering me, so he pulled off the lid. It was packed full of little slips of paper. Napkins, receipts, post it notes, half torn pages from notebooks and legal pads.

"You have an incredible voice," he said. "You should use it."

He leaned into me as he pressed the tin into my hands. He kissed me on the forehead. Then he turned and walked across the yard, got into his car, and started backing out of the drive.

I looked at the tin, fragments from my mind spilling over its edges.

"James?" I hollered, trying to shove the lid back on the tin. I ran to the car and he rolled his window down. "You are not invisible," I said. "I don't know what it is you expect for yourself, but you are anything but invisible."

He smiled sadly and nodded his head at me. I stood up and he rolled the rest of the way out the driveway. We both waved, and he was gone. Just like that. Gone from my life. I felt the weight of the tin in my arms, marveling that he had found a need to collect my musings all in one place like that.

Chapter 22

I slipped back into the house as quietly as possible. Joe was sleeping soundly on the couch beneath my mother's afghan. He was snoring just slightly, little puffs of air making his lips look pouty like a little boy.

I could hear the clink of a spoon slowly stirring a cup of tea. My parents were still in the kitchen. I imagined them sitting alert, listening, hurting from the words I had spoken to them only minutes earlier.

I slipped off my shoes and tip-toed up the stairs to my bedroom. I sat down on the floor and opened the lid to the tin. James had said I had a voice. I wanted to inspect the contents and see if I could hear it.

It was dark outside by the time my mother came upstairs. She knocked softly on my door frame. I looked up from the piles of scrap paper in front of me and invited her in with a nod of my head. She sat beside me on the floor and studied the uneven stacks of paper.

"What's this?" she finally asked.

"My voice," I said without explanation.

I could feel her watching me as I read through the slips of paper nearest me, and further divided them into smaller stacks.

"Ideas for fiction," I indicated the piles to my left, then swept my hand over the piles on my right. "And non-fiction."

"Writing," Mom said simply. It wasn't a question. It wasn't an answer. It was a statement, free from meaning or advice.

I could tell she was making a point of not reading what was on my slips of paper, and I found myself feeling very pleased by her effort.

Dad appeared at the doorway. "Joe's still sleeping pretty hard," he said. "I think he'll be okay down there for the night, but I'm thinking of moving him up to Zach's bedroom. He might sleep better." Dad came into my bedroom and sat down across from Mom and me.

"So... you shot Joe?" Dad asked. And so I told them the whole story. About the prints in the mud at Farmer Bob's place and how we'd run out of gas and followed the river bed until dark. I told them about Joe and I mistaking the bearded lady for the tigress, how we'd been a bit spooked to begin with and then how Joe had kind of thrown himself between us, thinking—I imagined—that he was saving me from the tigress, and how I hadn't even realized I'd hit Joe initially. He'd gone down silently. Well, I guessed he had roared first. There had been that terrible noise in all the confusion. And then Doc found us and filled Joe's truck with gas.

"I was a little afraid to take him to his place," I finished. "I just thought it would be better if someone kept an eye on him until he's fully awake. If anything, to explain to him where his last 24 hours have gone."

Both of my parents were nodding as if they agreed whole-heartedly.

I started stacking the fiction portion of my piles and, when I had them all together, I put them back into the cookie tin. Then I went to the stacks of boxes in the corner and found a nearly new notebook. I pulled that out and began stuffing the non-fiction sparks in, separating them by subject with blank pages. My parents just wordlessly watched my efforts.

"So I'd like to stay here," I finally said to them. "At least until I have a job and get some money saved. I'm thinking three months, six months at the longest."

"Of course," Mom said.

"You know you can stay as long as you need to," Dad said.

"But I have a condition," I added, just taking a moment to glance at each of their faces before completing my task.

"A condition," my father repeated.

"Yes. I stay here until I figure out which direction my compass is pointing, and we—none of us—pressure Zach about finding his direction."

The expected silence settled on us.

"I certainly don't want to pressure him," my father finally said.

I looked at my mother, waiting for her to answer. She was looking at the edges of my notebook, now stuffed with slips of paper, as if she expected my voice to start speaking to her from there.

"Of course not," she finally said.

"No pressure," I emphasized. "Not even if his gap year turns into two, or three, or more. Where Zach's path takes him is Zach's business."

Mom's eyes were looking a bit teary by the time she met my eye again.

"I'm so sorry, Jeni," she whispered. "I never meant to be so controlling. I thought I was doing what was best."

"I'm not blaming you, Mom," I interrupted. "I'm alright. Everything's going to turn out okay. For me. And for Zach. Just wait and see. Everything is going to be good."

When I came down to breakfast the next morning, Zach and Joe were eating scrambled eggs and bacon as my mother rushed to and from the kitchen with a skillet in her hand.

"Eggs?" she brightened when she saw me. This is where my mother went when she felt she'd lost her way. Her domesticity shone. She cooked meals that were twice as good and wore her apron with twice the enthusiasm.

Dad was sitting at the end of the table with his coffee in hand. He was reading the paper, but I could tell by the way his eyes weren't really moving across the page that he was using the newspaper as a barrier between himself and Joe. It was my father's way of building a little realm of safety. From behind the paper he could listen, observe, but avoid interacting unless he absolutely wanted to.

I sat down in the chair beside my dad and put my hand on his. He looked up and gave me a smile. "You look well rested," he said.

"Thanks, Daddy," I answered. I took a deep breath and faced Joe. "How are you feeling, Joe?" I asked.

Joe kind of grinned at me, but didn't slow down on forking up those eggs. "I was starving," he said. "But your dad got me started on coffee early this morning and your mom knows her way around a breakfast plate. I'm feeling surprisingly perky, considering." At this, he met my eye and I could see the smirk bubbling beneath the surface. "That's one heck of a bruise on my thigh," he added. "I don't know what I did to deserve it, but you sure got me a good one."

"That was for Orville," I said. "For rejecting all his offers of affection."

Joe laughed. My brother and my dad laughed. Mom came back into the room with a plate piled high with eggs and bacon. She sat it in front of me and then took her place at the end of the table.

"So tell us how the tiger hunt is going," she prompted my brother.

Joe and I both sat up a little straighter. We were eager to hear what was happening, as well.

"We heard her again last evening, but further off. "She's still on the move, and tame or not, I'm beginning to think she doesn't want to be found."

"What are they going to do?" I asked. "The circus schedule must be shot. Does the show go on without her?"

"Well, they're letting Giancomo out of jail," my father said. He turned the newspaper and tapped the story on the front page. "Circus Midget Found Not at Fault" the headline read.

Chapter 23

Half the town must have shown up to watch the circus leave town. Doc Stueve's parking lot was full and there were cars parked down the highway on both sides at least a half mile in each direction. Joe parked his truck in the clinic's driveway and Zach got out and lifted the orange tape that Doc must have strung at the last minute when he realized what an audience they were going to have. I jumped out of the truck too, and got in the bed to help hold the tape up over the truck.

I took out my camera and snapped pictures of the camels, the llamas and the lone circus giraffe. Orville saw me and knuckle walked his way across the drive. He posed prettily, then he stuck his tongue out at me, thumbed his nose, and turned away and smacked his rear.

Joe and Zach parked the truck and joined us, posing with Orville with the camels in the background. Rita came from around the back of Doc's shed riding a small white horse with a billowing mane. She was a picture, as always, and I snapped a few shots of her with my telephoto lens zoomed as close as I could get before she saw me. I saw my brother slip into quiet contemplation when he saw her. They waved at each other. She blew him a kiss and his cheeks turned pink.

Doc came out of his office with Giancomo. The midget and Doc made an odd enough pair, but the gathering crowd broke out in laughter when Orville joined the two of them. The midget stopped and spoke to Orville. The ape loped off, only to return shortly with a tall black hat and a bull horn.

"Ladies and Gentlemen of Dodge City," the midget bellowed. "I would like to thank you today for coming out, for showing your support. The circus is finally leaving town."

The crowd gave a half-hearted cheer.

"I know, I know. It's not every day that the circus comes to town in such a manner. Our otters run helter-skelter through your city streets, and our tigress makes the biggest disappearing act in circus history. Our star act, our dolphin, passed away in a field of Kansas wheat. I appreciate the support we've had through this difficult time. Your community has opened its arms to us, helped us care for our animals, and we've made some good friends as well."

The white horse with Rita on its back trotted up to the edge of the circle of people that had gathered round to listen.

"If you'll clear the path here, we'll get on with loading our animals," Giancamo's voice boomed.

Rita rode the pony up and down the area they were trying to clear. The crowd moved politely back, making a corral of bodies. My brother was at the gate for the camels. I supposed they could have backed the trucks up closer to load the animals, but Giancamo seemed determined to give the crowd at least a bit of a show.

When Zach opened the fence, the camels ambled out, walking in their kind of cross legged way, making their way to the largest trailer. The giraffe was straining her neck from the corral where she was still fenced. It was obvious she didn't want the camels going anywhere without her.

Rita rode the little pony into the pen where the camels had been. She climbed the tallest gate and beckoned to the giraffe. She clipped a long rope to its halter and then jumped back on the pony, unlatching the gate before trotting ahead. Unlike the camels, the giraffe moved quickly toward the trailer. Giancomo's grandson had shimmied up the side of the truck and was holding the top portion of the gate open. Rita let the rope drop and the giraffe hurried right in, bending its long neck as if to check that all its camel friends were there.

The crowd murmured in delight.

Rita's pony trotted back out. The pony reared and danced a small circle. Rita waved to the crowd who clapped appreciatively. Orville was working the crowd, as well, shaking hands, blowing raspberries, and grinning for photos. He took one man's hat, and when the orangutan offered to give the hat back, the man bowed low and offered it back to the great ape as a gift.

Orville hugged the hat to his chest gratefully, blew the man a kiss and moved on, working the crowd for more gifts and posing for more photos. By the time he reached me, he had a woman's pink scarf around his neck, a silver pair of sunglasses and a plastic daisy clenched between his teeth. At first I thought Orville was going to pass me right on by, but he stopped and stared at me solemnly. I put down my camera and offered my hand to Orville to shake.

"Goodbye, Friend," I said. Orville pulled me out into the clearing and put one hand on my shoulder and the other out, his way of asking me to dance. We did an odd little country two-step which ended in something of a tango. The crowd hooted and hollered and cheered us along. Then Orville held my hand and we walked together to Doc's shed where they were preparing to load the otters.

I couldn't help but laugh. The otters were like small puppies, so excited to go that they were bouncing at the door. Rita was off the pony. She and my brother carried small buckets of fish. Doc held the door for them to slip inside. We watched through the window as Rita tossed fish into a large carrying crate. The otters danced and spun and rushed in and out of their intended place. Finally, my brother dumped both his buckets into the traveling container, and the otters disappeared. Rita quickly shut the door and locked them in. Then I watched as Rita threw her arms around my brother and kissed him deeply. Orville and I turned away from the window. The ape looked at me knowingly, as if we both agreed they needed their privacy and it was up to us to protect it.

As the trucks were all loaded and the circus folks loaded themselves up, Giancomo got on the bullhorn once more.

"We shall return, Dodge City," he said gravelly. "The Meenling Brothers Circus will return and we will give Dodge City the show of the season. I am sorry to have met you all under such difficult circumstances, but we look forward to returning and showing you circus entertainment as it was meant to be."

Rita and Orville climbed into the big truck that Giancomo would apparently be driving. The crowd remained as the big circus trucks pulled out. We watched them leave Doc's parking lot and head south. Then the crowd began to dissipate until all that was left was me, my brother Zach, Doc Stueve and Joe standing in front of the clinic.

"Things sure are going to seem quiet around here," Doc said.

"No kidding," my brother agreed. I couldn't help but read a note of sadness to his tone.

"Oh, I don't know," said Joe. "The summer's barely begun and I've already been romantically pursued by an ape… and shot… that's more excitement than maybe all my summers thus far put together."

We all laughed.

"Doc? What about Lucy? What's going to happen to a tiger running loose in Kansas?"

"Ah, I imagine they'll catch up with her sooner or later," Doc said. "They've got every law enforcement officer from Colorado to

Nebraska to Oklahoma on alert. Chances are she's going to get too close to a farmer's herd of cattle one day soon and she'll be taken down. It's a shame we haven't been able to find her, but she don't belong in these parts. Her foreignness will catch up to her eventually."

"I don't think I'm done looking," Joe said. "I'd like to see her brought in alive rather than dead."

"I'm with you," my brother said, and we started planning our next tiger hunting expedition right then and there. Doc wished us luck and made us promise to keep him posted as to our target locations and findings.

"You get her, you give me a call," he said. "We'll make room for her here at Stueve's until the circus folk can come back for her," he said. "Don't be getting other locals involved. I don't want to see anything happen to her."

"You got it, Doc," said Joe. "And should I have any more trouble with the tranquilizer gun? I can call you for that, as well?"

"Of course," Doc laughed, then gave me a wink. "But boys, let's just be staying clear of Jeni's trigger finger, you hear?"

Later, alone with my brother in his little red pickup truck, I asked about Rita.

"She seemed kind of sweet on you. You got plans to keep in touch?" I asked.

My brother nodded. Something about the way he moved made me think of our father. He seemed older, somehow - older than even just a few days ago when I'd watched him walk across the stage for his high school graduation.

"She's really something," he said. "But I don't know. I could see myself getting a bit lost in Rita, you know what I mean? I'm not sure that I'm ready for a Rita in my life just yet." We rode in silence for a bit and my brother shrugged. "Maybe someday," he said. "We'll keep in touch, and maybe the timing will eventually be right for both of us."

I couldn't take my eyes off my little brother. "I don't know how you got so wise, Zach, but I sure wish you'd been advising me the past few years of my life."

"Hey," he said. "I don't think I ever thanked you for having my back. With Mom and Dad," he said. "I knew my gap year idea was going to be hard on them, and I'm glad you were there to provide a little support on my side of things."

I felt a little guilty. I didn't think I'd quite stood up to them, initially, enough to deserve any credit. I shrugged. "I was a good distraction," I said. "I gave them something else to dwell on. Together we divided their attention. Neither of us felt their full force since we were both being troublesome for the moment."

Zach held his hand up and I high-fived him.

"So how about you?" he asked. "Are you really going to stick around here for a while? Are you really coming back to Dodge City after working so hard to get the hell out of here?"

"Well, the way I figure it, this is where my trouble started," I said. "This is where I stopped listening to myself to begin with, so maybe it will be good to just be here for a while. Pick up where I started steering wrong, see if I can make it right for a while."

When we pulled into the driveway at home, Mom and Dad were sitting on the porch. Zach and I sat on the steps like when we were kids and we spent the whole evening laughing and talking and telling stories. It was the best time I'd had with my family in a very long time. I was home again. I was me again.

Chapter 24

One Year Later...

There is a postcard in my mailbox from my brother in Wales. I bring it into my apartment and tack it to the bulletin board where the world map hangs even though I know from his emails and his blog that he is now in London. He and I have a date to meet in Greece two weeks from today. It will be my first trip out of the county.

As well as my brother's blog, which chronicles his adventures backpacking across Europe, I follow Rita's. She's still with the circus, traveling the Midwest, but aside from Orville, they are almost an entirely human-driven conglomeration of acts these days. They've added aerialists and gymnasts, flexible folk and clowns. Rita has taken the marketing of a circus to a whole new level, almost like a television show the way she accounts for day-to-day happenings and behind-the-scenes looks at traveling with circus folk.

I'm living on the other side of town from Mom and Dad in a small, one-bedroom apartment that also serves as my writing studio. I've published one short story in a regional magazine in the year since I've returned home and am amassing a whole lot of rejections, but many with very kind, personal notes. The general consensus seems to be that they like my voice. I'm not always entirely sure, but I like the fact that I am finding it.

I'm working at the grocery store to pay the bills. I still prefer stocking shelves and working late at night when few people are in the store. It gives my mind time to wander and think about things that a more engaging job might not leave room for.

My cell phone buzzes and it's Joe, asking if I'm going to be available for pizza and a movie tomorrow night. We're dating, but it's casual for now. He occasionally gets all mushy and claims I'm the only girl for him, and I tell him he might just be the boy for me, as well, but we've got lots of time ahead of us and there is no hurry. I spend time with Lisa and am enjoying getting to know her kids.

Tiger Hunting

Tommy's not a bad guy either. He and Lisa can still be pretty mushy, at times, but I'm learning to appreciate the two of them together. I no longer feel like I lost a friend when Tommy and Lisa got together. I'm beginning to see that I've gained one.

I text Joe that I'll be back to town by four o'clock tomorrow afternoon and he can consider me all his after I've had time to take a shower. I finish packing my overnight bag and stuff extra batteries in my backpack. The last thing I do is pull a raw chicken out of the freezer and put it in a cooler which I then haul to the trunk of my car.

I've got three hours on the road before nightfall. I drive north and a bit east into the wilds of Kansas, passing one little town after another. If you're not from this area, you don't appreciate its beauty. It's true that the river beds are mostly dry, or have dwindled to measly streams, but what we lack in landscape around here we make up for in sky.

This is the spot Joe and Zach and I found last summer. This was where we consistently found her tracks and we heard her on more than one occasion. In spite of all our efforts, however, we'd been unable to locate Lucy the white tigress. By the end of the summer, Zach had saved enough money to start his travels and Joe was staying busier at the vet clinic since Doc Stueve had not yet hired anyone to replace my brother.

I pull off the highway onto a dirt road that leads me back along the riverbed. It's not a well-kept road, which makes it an ideal spot for what has become my ritual. I take a small tent and my sleeping bag a couple of times a month and I come here to camp on my own. I take my notebooks and my favorite pens and pencils. Sometimes I sketch and sometimes I write. I stay up late and marvel at the stars that blink above me.

She showed up the second time I made this trip on my own. Perhaps she was just too shy to reveal herself to my brother and Joe. Perhaps the three of us together made too much noise, forcing her to remain hidden. Perhaps she remembered me from that day when I'd been caught on my bicycle. Maybe I reminded her of Rita and, therefore, she'd been willing to let me know she was there.

On this night, she arrives earlier than usual. I hear the rumble of her purr before I see her, but I am no longer afraid. She approaches me on soft padded paws and sighs as she lets her body drop beside mine. I reach up and pet her massive head. She's a bit dirty, and still skinny compared to the circus posters she once starred in, but in general she looks good. She seems content, the same as I feel, to be relieved of performing for the moment.

"Aren't you lonely, Lucy?" I ask her. "Do you dream of India? Of other tigers?"

I worry about her. I watch the news incessantly, fearful that she'll be spotted and shot, or that she'll move from this rural neighborhood to hunt somebody's livestock. I've thought about turning her in, getting Doc Stueve and Joe up here to help me trap her at least a dozen times, and I imagine that very soon I will do this, but something in me resists. I don't want to think of her all caged up. I don't want to think of her put back on display in some circus or zoo. She'd never survive in the wilds of India, and while I suppose there is plenty of argument about why she doesn't belong here in the wilds of Kansas, for now it seems to be working for her.

I keep showing up with my bi-monthly gift of chicken. She will spend the night chomping and licking and purring her big rumbly purr beside me. We watch the stars together. I tell her about how I might be imaging my future with Joe and what I think I have learned about my past with James and about how it feels to be close to my parents again and how careful they've been to be supportive of me without criticizing.

I read her my stories. When I hear them out loud, I can often understand where I've missed the point or rambled on too long. I make notes on my papers in fine tipped markers by the light of a flashlight or by the light of the moon. Now and then I reach over and stroke Lucy's massive head. She's so soft and so warm that sometimes I imagine myself curling up next to her and drifting off to sleep. I remind myself that she's a wild animal, and unpredictable. I watch the way teeth go through chicken bone as if it's mere spineless hotdog. When I'm so tired I can't stay awake, I tell her goodnight and crawl into my tent to sleep. She's always gone by morning. The few nights I have stayed up all night and talked to her, she has left just before the breaking of dawn. She stands and stretches when the red streaks across the sky, but before the ball of orange rises to greet us.

I can't imagine what must be going through that big tiger head of hers, but something tells me that this is where she'd rather be. Given the choice of a circus or zoo, I think she has chosen the empty river beds of Kansas. Who am I to argue?

For now, I am in the place I have chosen, as well.

#

About the Author

Tracy Million Simmons was first published at age seven when her story, written on sheets of Big Chief Tablet, was taped to the center section of the coat closet in her second grade classroom for all to read. From that point on she has been addicted to words and paper.

She considers four years of work on the yearbook staff the most worthy pursuit of her high school career. After graduating from the University of Kansas with a degree in psychology, Tracy's first job was to create a series of aircraft maintenance manuals for ORBIS International, a non-profit organization bringing vision to the world through its flying eye hospital and educational programs. She went on to write letters for the organization, successfully acquiring millions of dollars of aircraft parts and medical donations. She also wrote and designed fundraising materials, newsletters and documentation for internal methods of operation and processes for the organization's administrators and staff.

Tracy eventually embarked on a freelance writing career that included feature articles in national and niche publications, ghostwritten material for busy doctors and dentists who needed a forum for connecting with their patients and sharing their expertise, website content generation for start-ups and established businesses alike, newsletter design, and line editing and rewrite services for self-published authors.

In 2003 she was the recipient of a mini-fellowship in fiction writing from the Kansas Arts Commission. In 2006 she received an honorable mention in the Kansas Voices Contest. She has been an active member of the Kansas Authors Club for more than ten years and is currently the editor of the organization's yearbook.

Tracy resides in Emporia, Kansas with her husband and three teenagers, all of whom she considers her muses, as well as her favorite people in the world to spend time with. She is the manager of the Emporia Farmers Market.

This is the first full-length novel that Tracy has written that does not remain in a box beneath the bed.

More about and by Tracy can be found online at
http://www.TracyMillionSimmons.com.